Being Clem

Being Clem

LESA CLINE-RANSOME

HOLIDAY HOUSE · NEW YORK

Library of Congress Cataloging-in-Publication Data

Names: Cline-Ransome, Lesa, author.
Title: Being Clem / Lesa Cline-Ransome.
Description: First edition. | New York : Holiday House, [2021]
Audience: Ages 8–12. | Audience: Grades 4–6. | Summary: When Clem's
father dies in the Port Chicago Disaster he is forced to navigate his
family's losses and struggles in 1940's Chicago.
Identifiers: LCCN 2020039122 | ISBN 9780823446049 (hardcover)
ISBN 9780823448968 (ebook)
Subjects: CYAC: Family life—Illinois—Chicago—Fiction.
African Americans—Fiction. | Single-parent families—Fiction.
Chicago (Ill.)—History—20th century—Fiction.
Classification: LCC PZ7.C622812 Be 2021 | DDC [Fic]—dc23
LC record available at https://lccn.loc.gov/2020039122

ISBN: 978-0-8234-4604-9 (hardcover)

For Linda and Bill Cline:
My first teachers and tormentors.
Agitators and allies.
My big sister and brother. My best friends.

Being Clem

ONE

There's 2,341 miles from Chicago to the San Francisco Bay. And even if you happened to catch a ride in one of those '44 Silver Streak Pontiacs with the shiny front grilles that look like big ole teeth smiling back at you, and drove as fast as the wind, it'd still take you about a week to get there. 2,341 miles is a lot of miles. But it ain't so far when an explosion that happens in San Francisco, California, lands right smack-dab in your lap here in Chicago.

I was sleeping good when that explosion happened. I heard loud knocking on the front door, and Momma's tired voice asking, "Who's that?"

I sat up in my bed, knowing there was no way company could be knocking on our door before Momma even called us in for breakfast. And then I heard her slippers scraping toward the door. Just as soon as Momma unhooked the chain and undid the bolt, all I heard after that was the screaming.

Soft-spoken is how most folks describe my momma. She speaks her mind, don't hold back on the truth, but she's just as quiet as can be. Before that night, I never so much as heard her raise her voice, let alone scream, but there she was, shouting like she was broken in two. By the time I hopped from my bed and made it to the front room where all the screaming was coming from, my sisters were already there, plus two men I'd never seen before, dressed just alike, holding their hats in their hands. They looked like the picture of my daddy my momma kept in a frame hanging over our kitchen table. *Soldiers.* They were holding up my momma by her arms. A piece of crumpled-up paper was lying on the floor in front of her. Her head was rolling from side to side. Clarisse, my oldest sister, put her hand out to stop me.

"Go on back to bed, Clem," she said, staring at Momma. But even she didn't sound like her usual mean self. So I stood there behind her watching our momma. It looked like her legs stopped working the way the soldiers had to hold her up.

"Get her some water, son," one of them said to me. But I was too afraid to move. I heard the water running in the faucet behind me and it was my other sister, Annette, filling up a glass. She brought it to the soldier, and he tried to get my momma to drink. Annette stood on the other side of me close.

Momma stopped screaming but her head was still rolling from side to side. Clarisse stepped away from me, toward the soldiers. We never had white folks in our house before, and these soldiers looked funny standing here in our living room holding up our momma.

"Do you have anyone you can ask to come over and sit with your momma till she's...uh, feeling better?" the soldier asked. But looking at Momma with her head rolling every which way, I didn't think my momma was ever gonna get right again.

"It's okay," Clarisse told him. "We'll be fine." She walked to our momma and sat her on the couch. I could see Momma's hand shaking in hers. Clarisse is only five years older than me, but talking to the soldier, and sitting on the couch calm as could be, she looked like the momma, and our momma looked like the child.

"Good evening, then," the soldier said to Momma, both of them tipping their hats to her. "Our deepest condolences."

Condolences. I had never once heard that word, but I knew as soon as the soldier said it, he was telling us he was sorry.

Over the next days I watched my momma sit still as a stone in that one spot Clarisse sat her in. I don't know who dressed her. Who combed her hair. How she did her business. She didn't look like she even remembered who I was.

Folks from our building and our church came in and out all day and night, whispering soft words away from Momma's ears, in the kitchen, where they left cakes and pies and chicken and sandwiches on the table. "Explosives…" and "They still don't know nothing…"

"Nothing to bury…," I heard one of the whisperers say.

My momma wore black, like any day now, we'd be going to a cemetery. Clarisse kept up her bossing, telling me and Annette to fetch this or get that or give Momma room to breathe when I tried to sit close to her and hold her hand and make her remember who I was. Reverend Maynard came over and prayed with Momma every day, and he might as well have been praying by himself. Momma sat with her head down, looking at her lap like it was the first time she'd seen it.

Finally, my momma's sisters, Aunt Dorcas and Aunt Bethel, came from Washington, D.C., and all of a sudden, they were like our momma's momma. They got her up off the couch and had Clarisse run some bathwater, "Hot as you can get it," they told her.

When our momma started her moaning and crying, they held her tight, with her face in their necks, letting her tears run down their dresses, shushing her with "C'mon, Cecille," and rocking her and rubbing her back like she was a little baby.

"Why does Momma have to be quiet if she wants to cry?" I whispered to Annette when they were busy shushing.

"Think they're afraid she'll start falling out, you know

how the ladies do in church when they get the spirit?" Annette whispered back.

That made sense to me, but Momma didn't look like the church ladies with their hands up in the air and their heads thrown back, praising. Momma looked like she even forgot who God was.

Next thing I knew, my aunts moved me out of my room while they moved in. Clarisse is fourteen years old, Annette thirteen, but the way they looked when I showed up at their bedroom door with my blanket and pillow from my bed, you'd have thought they had to share a room with a newborn baby instead of their nine-year-old brother.

"Aunt Dorcas said it's just till Momma gets better," I told them. Annette made room in her bed for me, but not before Clarisse rolled her eyes.

Our aunts got our momma eating and talking just a little bit again. One thing I know is, Clarisse didn't get her bossiness from our momma, but she sure got it from our aunts. It's like they bossed our momma back to herself again, and that was all I needed.

When I got up early one morning while everyone was still sleeping, I walked out to the front room and saw Momma sitting up on the couch.

"Clem?" she said so soft, I could barely hear her.

I walked over, making sure that was my momma talking,

and stared hard at her puffy face. She almost looked like the Momma before the soldiers knocked on our door weeks ago. She reached out and pulled me onto her lap. And even though I was too big to be sitting on anybody's lap, I let her hold me tight, and I rubbed her back, just like I saw my aunts do.

Later I found out it wasn't just my daddy who was killed in that explosion in San Francisco. There were 320 other navy men too. The Port Chicago Disaster, they called it. But didn't nobody bother to count the four of us, Clarisse, Annette, Momma, and me, here in Chicago. Because that explosion that happened 2,341 miles away just about ripped us apart too.

Before my daddy left this earth, I never thought much about him, and after he left, he was all I could think about.

Reverend Maynard held a service at Emmanuel Baptist Church for my daddy the first Sunday in August, same day as communion. They had every one of my daddy's pictures from our apartment up in front of the church on the pulpit, where the casket would have been if we had one.

Reverend Maynard preaches so long on Sunday Momma has to poke me with her elbow to keep me awake, but this Sunday I wondered if he finally ran out of things to say because it seemed like *bravery* and *honor* and *country* were the only words he knew. We sat in the front row, where the deacons usually sit, and even though it was hot, Momma, Clarisse, and Annette wore hats and gloves with their black dresses. The lace from Momma's glove scratched me when I held on to her hand, but I didn't let go.

After Reverend Maynard finished talking about what a good man our daddy was and after all the "amens" and "God bless hims" from everyone in the pews behind us, and after the choir sang, "Soon and very soon, we are going to see the king. Hallelujah, Hallelujah, we're going to see the king…," two soldiers walked up front and stood in front of us. They folded up a flag into a triangle and handed it to Momma. Momma didn't reach for it like she was supposed to, but Clarisse did and nodded to thank them. They saluted us and turned and walked back down the aisle and out the church doors.

Momma didn't do any more falling out like she did that first day we heard about the explosion, but she didn't do much of anything else either. She cooked, straightened up as best she could, always kissed us every morning and night. But she looked like she was half-asleep even when she was wide-awake.

I ain't like Clarisse and Annette and Momma. I don't remember much about my daddy. He went off to the navy before I could get too many memories of him in my head. If it wasn't for the pictures Momma keeps in the apartment, I might have even forgotten his face. But when I think of him,

I think of water. Of a big ole lake. I couldn't tell you if it was Lake Michigan or the Pacific Ocean, but Momma told me it was in South Carolina. And I remember it was hot.

Momma says my daddy was born on James Island with the Ashley River just down the road, and he grew up fishing with his daddy and granddaddy. He once told Momma he was on the water so much, it was land where he felt shaky. I remember he sat me tall on his shoulders and let the cool, muddy river water touch the bottoms of my feet. Daddy floated high in the water with me holding on tight to his neck. When he went low in the water, I heard Momma say, "Careful, Clemson, you'll scare him," but my daddy just laughed and kept right on ducking in and out till I started crying. He brought me back to my momma, and I watched him swim like a fish all around while Clarisse and Annette sat and splashed each other at the edge. After a while, Daddy dried off with a towel, and he made a fire and we all ate hot dogs and potato salad and drank soda pop on a blanket.

And I watched my daddy as he stuffed his mouth full of food and sat quiet looking out at the water. He reached over and held my momma's hand, and I was squeezed up between the two of them, but it didn't bother me at all.

Right before school was about to start up, I came in the kitchen and Momma was already up at the stove making breakfast.

"Morning, Momma," I said, hugging her around her waist.

She was quiet, kissed me on the top of my head, and went right on back stirring eggs.

I sat at the table, waiting to eat.

"Momma," I said.

"Yes, Clem." She didn't turn around.

"You ever want to be a spy?"

"Clem, I'm very tired," she said.

"But imagine if you went undercover as a double agent but as your disguise you were a cook behind enemy lines, and they loved your food. But one morning they came to breakfast, and you made your special eggs for breakfast, but they didn't know your special eggs had poison in them. And one by one, the special eggs with the poison killed off all the enemies we were fighting in the war. You could end the war just by making eggs."

My momma was quiet, but I could see her body shaking.

I jumped up from the table. "I'm sorry, Momma. I was just—"

She turned to me and her eyes were wet. She covered her mouth with her hand.

"Momma?"

She put her hand down and let out a loud laugh.

"Sit down, Clem, and eat your secret agent eggs," she

said, laughing some more. She was still laughing to herself when Clarisse and Annette came in.

"I think your brother is reading too many of his adventure stories," she said to them, fixing their plates. They looked at me with their eyebrows raised up.

Even though my momma was missing my daddy and half-asleep too, I knew now, if I tried hard enough, I could still make her laugh.

TWO

*C*lemson. It's a name that matches my daddy. Big, strong, and in charge. In the pictures of my daddy Momma keeps in frames in our apartment, in his sailor uniforms, he is standing tall over most of his navy friends on the docks or on boats out at sea. At Lincoln Elementary in every picture, from first grade on, they put me right up front, with the girls, so everyone can see that I'm just about the smallest in my class. *Clem.* It's a little bitty name. I never had any problems with my name until Clarisse started in on me, saying "Look at little Clementine." Clarisse took to calling me that until Momma made her stop. Now she only says it when Momma can't hear. But a clementine is just what I feel like sometimes. Small and sweet. But the picture of me in fourth grade is the one I can barely look at. In that picture, everyone, even the girls, were heads taller. Thinking back on that time, before Daddy passed, reminds me now of how just a year before he died, my momma wrote my daddy about all the goings on here in Chicago, and then everything happening with me and Clarisse and Annette. And how she was sure to mention, right at the end, how I was probably the smartest student at Lincoln Elementary, and Daddy wrote right back saying he wished he was as smart as I was, and could I please wait till he got back to graduate high school. Momma laughed when his letter came in the mail and she read that part aloud to us. But my daddy never came back. And he'd never see me or my sisters graduate from anywhere.

Out at recess, I ain't too bad at marbles, and I can hold my own in dodgeball, but most of the other boys in my grade made me feel as small as my name. In the classroom, sitting in the back, when the other boys didn't know the answers to Miss Schmidt's questions, and I could whisper the answers to them so soft and sideways out the corner of my mouth you'd think I was a ventriloquist, was the only time I felt strong. But I thought even that was going to stop when Miss Schmidt sent a letter home to Momma in my satchel. I just knew Momma was going to be some kind of mad.

"What does it say?" I asked her, standing, trying to read Miss Schmidt's curly writing behind Momma while she looked over the letter.

"Well," she said slow, answering while running her fingers under the sentences. "Miss Schmidt would like me to come in and speak with the principal."

"Am I in trouble?" I asked her, already knowing the answer.

"Why would you be in trouble, honey?" Momma asked, folding up the letter and looking at me.

When I didn't answer, she said, "Well, we'll find out what it is tomorrow."

The next day when I got home from school Momma was waiting for me. "Sit down," she said.

I put my head down.

"I won't do it no more," I told her.

"Do what?" she asked.

"Give out the answers," I told her.

"Clem, are you giving out answers in class to the other students?" Momma didn't look mad before, but now she did. I heard her taking God's name in vain under her breath.

"I see," she said. She sat quiet, looking at me look at the table. "I think you can put your talents to better use than that, don't you?"

She sounded like I bet my aunt Dorcas sounded talking to the students she taught in her high school history class. And I sure didn't want to think about Aunt Dorcas right now.

"I'm sorry, Momma."

She nodded. Seemed like that was all she needed, and then she said, "I went to see the principal today." I sat waiting for the part when the trouble was coming. "And both he and Miss Schmidt feel you are a very bright student," Momma said. "One of the brightest."

I looked up to see Momma smiling. "They want to move you to fourth grade."

"But I'm in third grade," I told Momma, thinking maybe she forgot.

"Yes, Clem, I know. But sometimes, people are smarter than the grade they are supposed to be in."

"And that's me?" I asked her.

"Yes, Clemson Thurber Junior, that's you."

"Clemson is a very special student," my new teacher, Miss Glynn, announced the day I walked into fourth grade. She put her arm around my shoulder and stood me in front of the class. "He has been moved from his third-grade class into our fourth grade. Let's give Clemson a—"

"Everyone calls me Clem," I told her.

She smiled down at me. "Of course. Let's give *Clem* a fourth-grade welcome," she said to the class.

It looked to me like not one of those fourth graders heard a word Miss Glynn told them about giving me a fourth-grade welcome, because from where I stood, the looks they gave weren't telling me to come on in. They were telling me to go back to third grade where I belonged.

"She sure he didn't come from first grade?" one of the girls up front whispered loud enough for me to hear.

After that first day, when I got home, I told Momma I wanted to go back to third grade.

"We can't always do what's easiest, Clem," she told me.

"Look at your daddy, and how brave he was in sacrificing for his country. Where would he be if he gave up every time he got scared?"

Alive? I thought to myself. But just as soon as I thought it, I took it back and asked God to forgive me.

So I thought about my daddy the second day I went back and listened to more of the "first grade" and "baby" talk. And I wondered if this was what bravery felt like, because it sure didn't feel good.

Miss Glynn sat me in the middle of the third row toward the back and I could barely see over the heads of the boys in front of me. But I could hear just fine, and even though now I was in fourth grade instead of third, I still thought the fourth-grade work wasn't much harder than the third-grade work, and I still knew the answers to most of the questions Miss Glynn asked. When the first test day came around, I felt a tap on my shoulder. "Hey, Professor, gimme the answer to number three." I could see my momma's mad face when I told her I gave out answers. But my momma wasn't sitting in a classroom with boys twice her size tapping on her shoulder. "Fifty-two," I whispered back.

Just like in third grade, before I knew it, there was a chorus behind me of "Ask Clems," and I'd have to pass back my whole doggone test to anybody who needed it.

"Hey, Professor!" they yelled at recess, rubbing my head

and patting my back, making me feel like a baby and a movie star at the same time.

I knew that giving away answers wasn't making my momma and daddy proud. But I also knew that being smart meant using your brain and that meant making it through fourth grade any way I could.

THREE

A nice Negro doctor is our landlord, and Momma says he and his wife are "good people." We only see them on rent day when he comes to collect. Before my daddy died, you could tell when it was rent day because Momma would put on her nicest housecoat, maybe a little bit of lipstick, and when we heard the knock on the door, she would talk just as sweet as could be to Dr. Stanford. Sometimes she'd invite him in for a cup of coffee, but he'd always say, "Oh, thank you, Mrs. Thurber, I'd love to, but I'll have to take a rain check."

"Why does he need to wait until it rains to have coffee?" I asked Momma. She just about bust a gut laughing when I asked that and told me it was a saying that meant "another time." But every month he said the same thing.

But the month after daddy died, Momma didn't put on her nice housecoat on rent day. She didn't even answer the door. When we heard the knock, Momma didn't move. She put her finger to her lips, which meant we all had to be quiet and pretend we weren't home like we sometimes did when we knew it was Mrs. Jefferson from the church who would come by right about suppertime and say she was "just passing by," but would stay and eat up all your food if you let her and never leave even when it got late and everybody was tired.

Momma says she's grateful Dr. Stanford only rents to "good, hardworking families," and we never had to live in a kitchenette apartment, all up on top of each other, sharing one bathroom with God knows how many folks.

"There's a lot I can abide, but I cannot abide that," Momma told us.

Here we have two bedrooms, the bigger one for Clarisse and Annette. The smaller one with the window looking down on the street is the one that used to be for me and Momma and Daddy. But after Daddy died, Momma took a quilt and pillow and started sleeping out in the front room on the couch and never came back. Now it's just a bedroom for me. And we have two big windows in the parlor that light up the front room in the mornings like a lightbulb, and a kitchen big enough for a table plus an icebox.

Just when we stopped seeing Dr. Stanford on rent day, I started seeing letters for Momma pushed under the door. I saw the first envelope pushed under the door with Momma's name written on the front early one morning on my way to the bathroom. I stopped and picked it up off the floor and put it on the kitchen table.

When I came in for breakfast, the letter was gone. "Did

you see the letter I left on the table?" I asked Momma. She shook her head, quiet. "Was it from your secret admirer?" I asked, smiling. I once read in one of Clarisse's romance magazines that boys sometimes slipped girls love letters if they really liked them but were too afraid to tell them.

"No, Clem, it was definitely not a secret admirer," Momma said in her tired voice. So I stopped asking and stopped smiling. I realized asking about a secret admirer probably made her sad thinking about Daddy.

When the second letter came, I left it in the same place and this time, I didn't ask any more about it.

Now other letters started coming too, and Clarisse let me know they were not from secret admirers.

"Bill collectors," she said, shaking her head and flipping through the mail one day when Momma wasn't home, like she was the daddy who was paying bills.

Momma had been looking for work for weeks, leaving the apartment early in the morning, all dressed up pretty with her hair fixed nice, wearing her church heels and shiny red lipstick. When Daddy was in the navy, Momma worked two days a week in the Emmanuel Baptist Church office typing up Sunday service programs and bulletins for Reverend Maynard. It was just her "spending money" job, she called it, and with the money Daddy sent home to Momma every month to pay our rent and bills, we had enough. Momma told us the U.S. government sent out a letter to every family of every soldier who died at Port Chicago, apologizing and telling them that they would make sure they were taken care of. That they would send them a check to "compensate" for their loss. Momma rolled her eyes when she said the word *compensate,* like it was a word the U.S. government made up. I didn't really know what that word meant, but I could tell by the way Momma said it that it had something to do with the government making a mistake by having the hundreds of Negro enlisted men load ammunition onto the ships without training them like they did the white soldiers who did it before them. And then when an accident happened, blowing up everyone in sight, blaming it on the Negro soldiers instead of the white officers in charge. All the money in the world can't make you forget about that. And how do you forget about your daddy dying because you have a check? Momma looked like she believed a check was coming about as much as she believed in the tooth fairy. So we had to go on living every day without waiting for "compensation."

With Daddy gone and just the little bit from her widow pension, and Momma not waiting on the compensation from Daddy's accident, Momma spent every day trying to find a secretary job like the one she has at the church. She got up early in the morning to take the el train all the way to the downtown Chicago office buildings where they hire for the secretary pool. And she said she had to smile extra pretty at white folks who probably threw away her application just as soon as she turned to walk out the door. Everybody knows can't no one tell whether a Negro or white woman types a letter, or makes an appointment or answers the phone, but Momma says that don't mean they want Negroes working in their offices. She says she has twice as much training as most of those white secretaries and could probably do twice the work too.

Now instead of two days a week, Momma was going to need to work the whole week to help pay the bills Daddy's money used to pay.

Every day Momma came home sweaty, with her lipstick nearly gone and her feet hurting, with no job. Made me go to bed thinking about if we were going to have to move to one of those kitchenette apartments with one room and share a bathroom with strangers.

"Can you work more days at the church?" I heard Annette asking Momma one night, while she took Momma's feet in her hands to rub the soreness out.

"Reverend Maynard said he could maybe give me one more day, but that's just not going to be enough. I'll figure something out, honey. Go on to bed," Momma told her.

I could hear the tired in my momma's voice all the way to my room.

"You look prettier than Lena Horne," I told her every morning before she left. Not just to make her feel better, but because she did.

"Thank you, Clem, but it's going to take a lot more than Lena Horne and a college degree to get a secretary job in Chicago," she said, smiling tired.

She asked our neighbor Mrs. Marshall to keep an eye on us while she was out looking, and Mrs. Marshall did her best but she's almost as old as Methuselah and fell asleep on the couch almost as soon as Momma closed the door. I knew if Momma walked in the door at the end of the day and her face was pinched up tight, not to ask how it went looking for a job, and not to start messing with Clarisse, just sit quiet until Momma got right. But one day, Momma came home and told us she got a job that she was starting on Monday morning, but her face was still pinched up tight.

"You did it, Momma." I went right over to hug her good, but she turned away.

"Not now, Clem," she said.

One thing I could always count on from my momma, even on the days when she was in her quiet moods or looking like she was half-asleep, was the way I could always make her happy just by hugging her or holding her hand like Annette or Clarisse couldn't. They always said I was her favorite, and

I always pretended like it wasn't true, but it was. At least it sure felt like it.

Momma was quiet at supper, and I could barely eat thinking if I couldn't make my momma happy, there must really be something wrong. Maybe my momma was sick and was gonna die too. Maybe Clarisse and Annette were sick and were gonna die. Those were about the worst things I could think of. I watched Momma close all through dinner, checking to see if she looked sick. She looked about the same, but I didn't know if she was just trying to look strong to keep it from me. After she washed up the dishes, dried and put them away, and she still didn't want nothing to do with me, I went into my room and laid on my bed. Clarisse called me a baby nearly every day. And I know crying doesn't make anybody a baby, but I couldn't stop the tears from coming then. I cried so hard I didn't hear the knocking and didn't hear Annette walk in. When I opened my eyes, she was looking down at me.

"You okay, Clem?"

I had snot running out my nose, and I had to wipe it on my bedsheet.

"Is Momma going to die?"

Annette looked at me like I was crazy. "No. Of course not," she said.

"Are you or Clarisse going to die?" I asked her.

"Clem, no one is dying," Annette told me. "Momma is just upset is all."

"About being sick?"

"Move over," she said, shoving me to the side while she laid down next to me. That made me cry some more. "C'mon, Clem," she told me, and I could tell from her voice that that meant to stop my crying, and stop acting like a baby, so I stopped.

"She's feeling sad," Annette told me.

"About me?" I asked her.

"Now why would Momma be sad about her little Clem?" Annette asked.

"You sound like Clarisse when you talk like that," I told her.

"Sorry," she said. "But no, she ain't sick, and she ain't sad about you. She's sad 'cause she has to work a job she don't want to work."

I turned on my side to look at her. Annette doesn't talk nearly as much as me and Clarisse. Some days Annette don't say much at all, but I think that while we're fussing and talking, Annette must be watching and listening. "How do you know that?" I asked her.

She turned on her side and looked at me. She smiled the

same tired smile Momma does when she doesn't feel like explaining something that shouldn't need explaining.

"Because I know, Clem."

"You sure she's not mad at me?" I asked her.

She smiled big now. "How could anyone be mad at our little Clem?"

FOUR

The first day my momma started her new job was the second time I saw her cry. I came in the kitchen and her hands were laid flat on the ironing board and her shoulders were up around her neck. "Momma?"

She turned then, trying to smile. She took a handkerchief out of her housecoat and started dabbing at her eyes.

"You okay?" I asked her. I could see clear as day she was crying and sniffing, but I was wanting her to be okay, so I asked hoping she'd tell me a lie. And she did.

"Yes, Clem, I'm fine. Your eggs are on the stove, honey." The Japanese could drop another of those bombs in the middle of Michigan Avenue and my mother would say, "Don't forget to eat your toast, baby."

I pulled up a chair and ate my eggs while me and my momma pretended she was just fine. She took out a gray dress from a bag and put some starch on the white collar and pressed it with the hot iron so it was as stiff as a board. Then she sprayed water on the dress and pressed each part, the puffy sleeves, the pleated skirt, real slow.

"You have to wear that to your new job?" I asked her with my mouth full of eggs.

My momma didn't turn around. So I asked again.

"Momma?"

I stopped eating.

I walked to the ironing board and stood in front of Momma and watched her ironing the same part of the dress again and again.

"Momma, that's already pressed good," I told her.

"Go sit down, Clem," she said.

"But Momm—"

"Go sit down," she said, her voice almost as sharp as Clarisse's. She was still pressing the same spot. I didn't move.

I put my hand on hers and could feel the wet steam making both our hands wet as she kept moving the iron back and forth. She started ironing faster, wiping her eyes at the same time.

I dried my hand on my pants, left the kitchen, and went straight to Clarisse and Annette's room.

Clarisse was sitting up in bed taking the rollers out of her hair. I didn't like to mess with her too early in the morning, so I went to Annette's bed even though she was still sleeping.

"Get out of here, Clem!" Clarisse yelled before I closed the door to their room behind me.

"Something's wrong with Momma," I said, standing over Annette, trying to shake her awake. I knew trying to wake up Annette could take a while, so I pinched her arm to hurry it up.

"What's wrong, baby boy?" Clarisse started in on me. "Mommy didn't warm your milk this morning?"

I tried again with Annette. Finally, she opened her eyes.

"Clem?" she said, her eyes half-open. "What's wrong?"

"Why do you all baby him so much?" Clarisse yelled.

"Something's wrong with Momma," I told Annette. "Come see." I pulled Annette to her feet and we walked to the kitchen. Momma hadn't moved from the ironing board.

"Momma, you okay?" Annette asked her real sweet.

"There's eggs on the stove," Momma said.

Annette looked at me and shrugged.

I acted out ironing with my hands and pointed at Momma.

Annette stood and watched.

"Momma, you finished pressing that uniform," she said, and went over to take the iron. But Momma held it up high, almost over her head. Annette stepped back quick.

"Momma, be careful!"

Clarisse walked in. "What's going on?"

"I think Momma needs to sit down for a minute," Annette told her, not taking her eyes off Momma.

Clarisse looked from Annette to Momma. From Momma to me. From me to the iron spitting out steam. From the iron to Momma. She took three steps and took the iron from Momma's hand, put it down on the ironing board, and sat Momma down in a chair at the table while me and Annette stood watching.

If the navy ever needs women soldiers to fight along with the men, Clarisse will be the first one I'll sign up.

"Here, Momma, take a sip of your coffee." Clarisse put Momma's coffee cup to her lips, but Momma turned her head. Clarisse looked at Momma sideways.

Clarisse still had half the curlers in the back of her head, and I could see through her worn-out flowered nightgown. On any other day, I would have had about a million and one jokes, but today, I couldn't think of one. She sat down across from Momma. Me and Annette stood behind her.

"Momma," Clarisse said to Momma like she was talking to a child.

Momma looked up at her.

"Momma, they're expecting you at work today."

"I know that, Clarisse." Momma sounded so tired.

"Your uniform is all ironed, and it's time to get dressed."

"I know that, Clarisse."

Hearing Momma repeat the same words over and over made the eggs in my stomach start bubbling around.

"Do you want me to help you get dressed?"

"Now why would I want you to help me get dressed?"

Momma asked like it was Clarisse that wasn't right in the head.

Clarisse turned and looked at us. Annette shrugged.

"Well, okay then. Let's all get a move on," Clarisse said. "Clem, could you get your dusty behind dressed, please?" she added, pretending it was just any regular day.

She handed Momma her uniform from the ironing board, and Momma looked like it had snakes crawling all over it. But Clarisse pushed it into her hand again, wrinkling it. Momma didn't even notice.

"Get dressed, Momma," Clarisse said, looking her in the eyes. It was one of the only mornings where there was no fussing getting out of the house. Me, Annette, and Clarisse got dressed quick and stood at the door waiting, it seemed like for hours. Just when Clarisse was about to call out "Momma" again, Momma walked out of the bathroom with her uniform on.

She didn't look at us but went straight to the front closet, put on her coat, took her purse, kissed each of us goodbye, and left for her first day working for the Franklin family in Hyde Park as their maid.

FIVE

With Momma working during the day at the Franklins', I got to spend a lot more time with Annette and Clarisse.

"When you get home from school, get yourselves something to eat and start in on your schoolwork," Momma said. "Clarisse, I may need you to get dinner started on Thursdays. Mrs. Franklin said those are gonna be my late nights." Clarisse was looking down at her fingernails.

"Clarisse is gonna cook? Momma, are you trying to kill us?" I asked, laughing. But Momma didn't want to hear any of my jokes tonight. I'd never seen her look so serious. She had us lined up on the couch and was giving directions like she was a drill sergeant and we were recruits.

"Annette, I'd like you to get the floors swept and mopped on Fridays before I get home. And help out Clarisse as best as you can."

"What am I gonna do, Momma?" I asked.

Momma looked down at me hard. "You just focus on getting home after school, Clem. The work in fifth grade is challenging so just get your schoolwork done," she said.

"You mean because he can't do anything else?" Clarisse asked Momma, sweet as could be.

Momma frowned at both of us. "No, it's just that...well, Clem, you need to make sure you keep your grades up," she said.

"Me and Annette don't need to keep *our* grades up?" Clarisse asked.

"You know what I mean," Momma said. But I didn't know what Momma meant. I was glad to not have to cook dinner or mop the floor, but somehow not having anything to do made me feel like nobody needed me for anything.

"And absolutely no company in this house while I'm not here. Is that understood?" When Momma said this, she looked right at Clarisse. We all nodded, but it was usually just Clarisse's friends that came over. All of them pretty and loud-talking like Clarisse. It was like Clarisse went and started a Bossy Girl Club at DuSable High School, and her friends were all members. They came in like it was their house, dropping down their purses and taking up all the space. The whole house smelled like perfume and girl sweat and bubble gum. They talked loud, played the radio loud, and if I came out of my room, they teased me loud just like Clarisse did.

"Ooooh, it's little Clem," the big one named Sherry always said whenever she spotted me. "Come here, Clem, and give me a hug." I always ignored her and kept on walking to the kitchen or bathroom or wherever else I was going, listening to the sounds of them behind me. "I don't think your brother likes me," Sherry would say, laughing, and Clarisse would join in. I hated those girls and their loud-talking ways. Annette told me to pay them no mind.

"They're just playing with you, Clem," she said.

Best thing about Momma being at work was I didn't have to hear the Bossy Girl Club anymore, now I only had to deal with the president, Clarisse.

Not two weeks after Momma sat us down like new recruits going over the rules, I came home from school and thought Clarisse had turned on the radio and was having herself a party in the kitchen. Annette had club meetings sometimes after school, and those were the days Clarisse had the house all to herself for just a little while till I got home. I was making my way into the kitchen to break up her party when I first smelled the perfume and then heard my least-favorite voice saying,

"Girl, don't get me started…"

Sherry.

I had barely closed the door when Annette came in behind me. She looked right at me, then looked at the kitchen where all the noise was coming from. Annette took off, fast as Jesse Owens. Next thing I knew the Bossy Girl Club came running out of the kitchen and into the front room, grabbing their coats and yelling, "Relax, Annette," and "Dang, you ain't nobody's momma."

Clarisse was just standing there looking like she was going to kill Annette first chance she got, but when everyone finally left and the door closed, Clarisse turned to Annette and opened her mouth.

Annette put up her hand. "Save it, Clarisse. Momma doesn't ask much, just don't have people up in this house while she's not here. You got a problem with that, take it up with Momma."

Clarisse closed her mouth, and Annette walked into the bathroom and shut the door.

"What are you looking at, Clementine?" Clarisse yelled. Now she was mad at me, probably thinking I told on her to Annette. I don't know what Annette and Clarisse said to each other later that night, but Clarisse never had her friends over again.

I know my momma kinda said Clarisse was in charge when she wasn't there, but now Clarisse took it too far. From the time I walked in the door, there she was, "Take off your shoes," or "Wash your hands," or "Don't even think about another bite until you finish your schoolwork." Like it was her job now to show me how to follow the rules. But even our own momma was never this bad.

As mad as I sometimes was at Clarisse for bossing me, I was proud too for the way she stepped in, cooking meals when Momma had to stay late or go to her NAACP meetings. Turned out Mrs. Franklin asked Momma to stay late a lot more than Thursdays. Seemed like every other week she was staying late for one reason or another, and every time it would be past the hour when Momma was supposed to be home and we didn't hear her dragging slow up the stairs, Clarisse would start taking things out of the icebox to make dinner. Now, Clarisse ain't no kind of cook, but she did all right. And Annette did just like Momma said with sweeping up, but she did even more. The house was almost always neat. I think it hurt Annette to have Momma have to come home and even wash a dish after doing for white folks all day long, so she cleaned our apartment like she was the Thurber family maid. But me, all I did was do my schoolwork, watch everybody else work, and wish just once, someone would treat me like I had something to offer.

SIX

Me and Momma both like to get up along with the sun, before Chicago gets going good. For most of the day, Chicago is about the loudest place on earth, with car horns honking and the el training rattling overhead, but early in the morning, it seems like me and Momma are about the only ones up and about, and it's as still and silent as that time I barely remember when I visited my daddy's folks in South Carolina. Of course, then I thought I was about to lose my mind with the same nothing sounds every day, but by the time we left and we were driving back to Chicago, I was missing those nothing sounds.

In the early mornings in our apartment, sometimes my momma seemed miles away from Prairie Avenue. I didn't know where she went when she sat quiet, looking out the window, but sometimes it looked like she'd never find her way back. But sitting quiet by herself was when I could tell she missed Daddy the most. I almost felt jealous, wishing I had memories of my daddy so big and strong, they could carry me as far away as the places on my maps. But only Momma had those, and it seemed like she wanted to keep them all to herself.

But the mornings when Momma was the quietest were the mornings when she sat at the kitchen table to pay the bills. The envelopes were sitting in a stack and Momma kept a big pad of paper and a pencil next to her and did a lot of scratching and erasing.

On those mornings, listening to the scratch-scratching of her pencil and every once in a while hearing her breathe in deep and slow, I knew not to say one word, not even ask a question. I just pretended to be busy eating or drawing, but I was really watching Momma with her head in her hand, adding and erasing rows of numbers on that pad of paper. It looked to me like maybe Momma was not so good with math because the numbers never seemed to add up right, and she shook her head and had to start all over again.

Once there was so much erasing, I couldn't help myself and asked, "You need help with the math, Momma?" thinking I was probably better at adding up the numbers than she was.

She shook her head, staring at the paper. "It's not the math I need help with, Clem," she said with her lips tight.

Momma, Clarisse, and Annette didn't tell me much, but I could tell Momma was buying less food, and even though she used to buy a pretty dress or nylons with the seam up the back, or a new hat for church service, she never bought anything nice for herself anymore. Instead of buying dresses from the store for Clarisse and Annette like she used to, she bought fabric and patterns to make their dresses.

"This will be fun. We'll be like famous fashion designers, making our dresses," Momma said, trying to sound like this was what she wanted all along.

Later that night, when Momma was in the kitchen, Clarisse wrinkled up her nose at the idea of wearing dresses Momma made at home, and I heard her whisper to Annette, "I'd rather go to school *naked* than wear some old homemade dress."

"Then you're gonna be cold come winter," I heard Annette say back to her. I loved Annette more than ever then.

Something told me that Momma couldn't make numbers add up on paper when she didn't have the money in her purse. All of a sudden, things I never once thought about, I couldn't stop thinking about. I knew plenty of people at school who lived in parts of Chicago Momma told me weren't safe and to stay away from. Now we were gonna be their neighbors, living in a kitchenette apartment with Annette and Clarisse going to school wearing homemade clothes or going naked. Here was my momma, who went to college, and me, skipped a grade, and Annette and Clarisse, who were smart too in their own way, and between us we were doing worse than ever without my daddy.

I didn't have to be good at math to know wasn't none of this adding up. What good was being smart if you couldn't figure out how to keep a roof over your head or food on the table? But more than anything else, I wondered why no one thought I had a right to know what was going on. It was like there was a secret club of Thurbers, only they forgot to invite me to the meetings.

SEVEN

On the mornings when it was just me and my momma visiting my daddy in her faraway place, she would all of a sudden come back to Prairie Avenue, just like that, saying something like, "Clem, would you go and make sure your sisters are up, baby?" and then she was Momma again. She didn't mind me being up, sitting with her at the table, reading or copying maps from my books, as long as I could do it "quietly." Sitting quietly ain't my favorite thing to do. One morning when my momma told me I ask questions like I'm a private eye, I knew she was telling me to stop with my talking, so I sat with my mouth shut. I know Momma felt bad talking mean. But she turned and went back to looking out the window, and I nearly had to bite my tongue to keep from asking just one more question and let her be until she came back to Chicago.

Today Momma stood at the ironing board in her housecoat pressing her clothes while I ate my oatmeal.

"I'm going to be a little late tonight, baby," Momma said, the steam from the iron floating up over her head.

"Why? It ain't Thursday," I said, not looking up from

my book. And I sure didn't need to remind my momma how many extra late nights she worked, because on those nights when the Franklins kept her too late for "just one last thing," Momma was barely in the front door before she started in.

"…not respecting my time," she'd mumble before she even hung up her coat. "'Just a few more minutes, CeeCee,'" she'd say, sounding just like Mrs. Franklin in her white people voice.

Momma laughed. "No, not the Franklins tonight. It's an N-A-double-A-C-P meeting." For the life of me I can't ever remember what those letters stand for, but I know it has something to do with colored folks, important business, and making changes. Behind Momma's back, Clarisse calls it the N-A-double-A-B-C-P meetings, "the National Association of *the Best* Colored People," but she only says that to me and Annette.

One time, Annette said in my ear after Clarisse left the room, "I'm surprised *she* ain't the president." We just about bust a gut laughing.

"I left some sandwiches in the icebox for dinner," Momma said.

"Momma!"

Here we go. I tried to shove the last of the oatmeal in my mouth before Clarisse came in.

"Momma, where's my skirt?" Clarisse looked at me. "I can smell you from here, Clem. Momma, does he ever take a bath?"

I grabbed my book and breathed oatmeal breath all in her face as I passed her in the doorway. "Momma!" she yelled.

"Please, don't start," Momma said, smiling at me behind Clarisse's back. "I just pressed it, Clarisse." She pointed to the back of the chair, where she had hung the skirt on a wooden hanger, with every pleat pressed sharp as a knife.

I knew the Franklins paid Momma to be their maid, but far as I knew Clarisse wasn't paying our momma to be hers.

"Why can't you iron your own skirt?" I asked her, ducking fast before she hit me.

"Mind your business, baby boy," Clarisse said.

"Annette," Momma called out to the back bedroom, not paying any attention to me or Clarisse. "C'mon, let's get moving, baby." No matter what happens, Annette is not going to rush for anyone.

Momma got dressed in the bathroom while they ate in the kitchen, and we all left out together. She liked to kiss each one of us goodbye at the door, though I could see Clarisse turn her head so Momma couldn't kiss her good. Momma acted like she didn't notice. They went on ahead downstairs, Momma to the streetcar, Clarisse and Annette walking to meet their friends on the corner of Forty-Fourth and Michigan, and then they walked over to DuSable High School. But I stopped on the next floor and went to apartment 2B and knocked. I could hear the sound of a man's loud snoring from outside the door. I knocked a little harder. Finally, the door opened and standing there looking at me cockeyed was Errol.

EIGHT

I know Momma felt bad about me being a boy and not having a daddy around. Not even a brother to talk to. And I know she was hoping Errol could be a kind of a brother to me. But if that's what she was wishing, she might as well have been waiting on a genie with a magic lantern because me and Errol being like brothers was never going to happen. Just like family, me and Errol never had a choice about whether or not we wanted each other's company. Being together was just the way it had to be.

Seemed as soon as Errol and his family moved into our building, our mothers met, standing side by side in the cold, waiting on the streetcar. Coming home, they got off on the very same streetcar at the very same time and walked home together. And just like women do, it wasn't too long before it was, "Ooh, I have a son just about that age," and "Ooh, I work for a family over in Hyde Park too." Sometimes it seems to me that you only need to be a woman to start telling each other all your business just as soon as you meet. Next thing I knew Mrs. Watkins was up in our apartment every night at our kitchen table like she was a paying boarder. She'd stay there so long, Errol's daddy would make his way upstairs, start pounding on our door, asking if Mrs. Watkins forgot she had a family downstairs to look after. And then Mrs. Watkins would get all red in the face and say, "Thank you, Cecille, I'll be getting on now," but rolling her eyes at the same time, and they would laugh some more.

After a while, Mrs. Watkins started bringing up Errol so she could sit and talk a little longer.

"You boys go on and play," Momma would say. But you can't play with someone who don't say but two words to you.

When they'd get to the apartment, Mrs. Watkins would say to Errol, "Do you wanna go on and show Clemson the new army men I bought you?" and he'd say something only she could hear.

"Errol left them downstairs," she'd tell us, like he'd said it clear as day. Or she'd ask him "You want something to eat?" And then she'd tell my momma, "He ain't hungry yet."

I once asked my momma if Mrs. Watkins was a mind reader like the one we saw in the tent every summer at the South Side circus who can tell what you're thinking just by looking in your eyes, because she sure seemed to know everything in Errol's head.

"Just give him time to warm up, Clem," she told me.

Being friends with Errol was like going onstage every day as Edgar Bergen and putting my hand in the back of his Charlie McCarthy doll and making him talk. Only I wasn't no ventriloquist, and Errol wasn't no dummy. At least not a wooden one.

"What time is it?" Errol asked me, holding the door with his hair half combed.

"Well…" I pretended I was looking at my wristwatch. "Looks like it's about a quarter till late." Errol's about the only person I know slower than Annette. I begged my momma to let me walk to school by myself, but she said it's safer two boys going on to school together. Even if it takes a little bit longer to get there.

"Just a minute," he said, same as he said every morning, and went back inside. He came out with his army sack on his back, coat over his arm, his hair combed almost all the way through, holding his lunch sack, and locked up with the key hanging from a chain around his neck. But now his shirt was untucked and he had dried milk on his top lip.

"Mirror, mirror, on the wall, who's the crustiest Negro I know?" I said. He looked at me like I was speaking martian.

I shook my head. "You break another mirror?" I laughed. "'Cause you sure ain't looked in one this morning." Errol just stared at me. I wiped at my mouth. And then he wiped his, cleaning it off. I didn't bother to tell him about his shirt.

Outside it was loud again, like a Chicago morning. The el train rolled above us all the way down Calumet Avenue, riding till we turned onto Forty-First Street.

I walked on ahead. I might have to walk with Errol, but it didn't mean I had to walk beside him. At the corner, the door to Miss Pearl's Luncheonette was open and the morning smells of coffee, bacon, and cigarette smoke met me on the sidewalk. Each booth was filled with men at tables reading papers and eating plates piled high with food. I stopped and waited for Errol.

"That's enough to make you lose your appetite." I pointed to a man sitting on a stool, with his shirt rolled up high and his pants hanging so low in the back we could see just about half of his behind. Errol laughed loud enough for the man to look up from his plate and over at us.

We kept on and Errol was still walking slow. Even the cold doesn't make him pick up his step. Our teacher, Miss Cosgrove, wasn't so bad as far as teachers go, but sooner or later, even she was going to get tired of seeing me and Errol coming in just before the bell rang nearly every single morning.

NINE

There's quiet and then there's Errol. There were kids in my classroom that were too scared to raise their hand. Some didn't say a peep all day. They were quiet. Errol just didn't have anything to say. When he was visiting with his momma, those were the times I was glad when Annette and Clarisse were around. They'd come in, talking loud. "What are you all doing?" they'd ask us, when they could see clear as day we weren't doing nothing at all.

They'd tell Errol how cute he was. Tell Errol how ugly and what a pain in the behind I was. He'd smile a little then. I knew he had older brothers, moved on now, working factory jobs not far from Chicago in Beloit, I heard Mrs. Watkins tell my momma. And maybe, before they left, they talked as much mess about him as my sisters did about me now.

Errol thought I didn't notice the way his eyes stayed on Clarisse every time she walked in the room. The way he laughed extra hard at everything she said. Like he was *in love*.

"You thinking about asking Clarisse to marry you or what?" I asked him one day when he was looking extra in love.

"You're crazy," he said, looking down at his feet. And I knew that meant, yes, Errol *was* in love with Clarisse.

Our mommas made us stick together, so that's what we did. I was stuck with Errol at home and at school, sitting together at lunch or standing together on the playground. After "Professor," "ClemandErrol" was my other name.

If Mrs. Watkins was visiting, the loud street sounds outside my window were quieter than the sounds from the kitchen when I laid in bed at night.

Outside my door, I could hear Momma laughing the way I imagine she used to laugh when she was with her sisters, or back when my daddy was still alive. And I could hear their whispering too, almost like Clarisse and Annette do when they have secret things to talk about.

But one night, instead of the laughing and whispering, all I heard was crying. I got up out of the bed and went and listened close at the door when I thought it was Momma's crying. But even after I heard Momma's voice and knew it was Mrs. Watkins who was crying, I stayed at my door listening.

"C'mon now, Beulah. Let me take a look," I heard Momma's voice say soft and deep at the same time.

The crying quieted down a bit, and Momma's voice got softer.

"You know this doesn't make any kind of sense," she

said. "You don't have to put up with—" and the crying started again.

Now that I was up and listening, I had to go to the bathroom, but I was afraid Momma would get mad and think I was listening in on their talking, even though I was, so I had to hold it.

That whispering and crying went on and on until I just about thought I was going to wet myself, and finally I heard the front door close.

I waited until I heard the water in the kitchen sink running before I opened my door to run to the bathroom. I had to pass Momma in the kitchen to get there and on my way, I heard Momma talking to the dishes. "Needs to keep his hands to himself…," she said, slamming the coffee cups in the sink hard enough to break. All of a sudden, I didn't have to go to the bathroom anymore.

"Momma." I said, coming up on her slow, not wanting her to slam anything harder.

She turned quick. "Oh, Clem, baby. You scared me." She put down the washrag and turned off the water. "What are you still doing up?"

"I had to go to the bathroom," I started, but finished in my head, *but then you and Mrs. Watkins were out here raising the dead with the crying and dish slamming…*

"Well, hurry up and go on back to bed, honey. It's late," she told me.

"Everything okay with Mrs. Watkins?" I asked her.

Her face got tight, but she smiled. "Of course it is, baby. Go on to the bathroom, Clem," she said, telling me there wasn't no more room for my questions.

I went in and ran the water, but still I didn't have to go, so I went on back to bed.

It was quiet now outside and inside, and I laid there and thought about my daddy, trying again to see his face that day at the lake. And thinking how he held onto Momma's hand. But every time I thought about his hand holding tight to hers, I could see Errol's daddy too, mad about Mrs. Watkins spending so much time in our apartment talking to Momma. Mad about having to do for himself. I wondered if he was mad at Errol too. Here was my daddy gone, and his daddy living right downstairs, and now I didn't know which was worse.

TEN

Every year, as much as I loved being in school, when it got to be around June, summer couldn't come fast enough. Having more time to go to the library was one reason. Another was that every summer our momma would send me and my sisters to stay with our aunts in Washington, D.C., for "summer enrichment camp," she called it. Of course Clarisse called it "summer prison camp." Sometimes Momma took us on the train, but if our aunts decided to visit friends in Chicago or go to one of their big Negro Women's group conferences, they would come and take us back with them to D.C. on the train.

In Washington, D.C., Aunt Dorcas and Aunt Bethel never had children of their own, and they think they can practice being mommas to us, but being a practice momma ain't the same as being a real momma, especially when being a practice momma means spending all day bossing us and making us pick up after ourselves and see "important historic monuments." They told Momma I was a handful, but it was good to get out of Chicago for a bit.

The only time we missed a "summer enrichment camp," was the summer Daddy died. But the next summer, we made up for it with two trips. The first was the usual one to Washington, D.C., and then our uncle told Momma to send us down to visit our cousins. We came home for a week in between, so Momma could take us back on the train for a short ride to visit our cousins in Milwaukee, the children of my daddy's only brother, Uncle Kent. I felt like a world traveler, heading back and forth from one train station to the next. Uncle Kent seemed like he had about a million kids in his little house on Townsend Street. They were loud and rowdy, but I don't know when I had a better time. We slept all on top of each other, just arms and legs everywhere. Even with all the windows open and a little bitty fan in the corner, you couldn't even get a breeze, but nobody cared because we were cousins and the next morning when we got up, there would be breakfast waiting, and after we washed up and pulled on some clothes, Aunt Thea and Uncle Kent didn't mind how long we stayed outside as long we didn't get hurt or hurt no one else. All Uncle Kent's children had names that started with the letter *K,* just like Uncle Kent's, like they ran out of ideas for names. The oldest was Kandace, just two years older than Clarisse. Then there was Kent Junior, one year older than Clarisse, who everyone called K.J. and looked the most like Uncle Kent, and Kara Ann who was one year younger than Annette. Kendrick was one year older than me and Kelvin was two years younger. You would think Uncle

Kent and Aunt Thea would mix their names up as bad as me and Clarisse and Annette did, but they never did. I even heard Aunt Thea in the kitchen call out once, "Get in here, K!" and I couldn't wait to see who would answer.

Of all my cousins, it was Kendrick I liked the best and not just because we were the closest in age. It was because he always had the best ideas. Some days it would be so hot sitting on the front porch, it seemed like your brain was frying, and we would stretch out, just about sweating ourselves to death, and it would be Kendrick who would say, "Wanna go see if we can sneak into the pool downtown?" Or after dinner, when the girls were washing up dishes, Kendrick would whisper in my ear that he could show me a place where he heard a little girl who lived down the street once disappeared into thin air. "Her parents never saw her again," he told me, and it made the back of my neck itch. I let him pull my arm and drag me off the porch and down the street. I was half believing what he said, and one half of me wanted to stay on the porch safe and sound, but the other half wanted to see if what he said was true.

When Kendrick saw me thinking too hard about if something was a good idea or not, or getting scared like I do about getting hurt or in trouble, he'd say, "You can't keep waiting on someone to give you permission. A man jumps in first and thinks about it later."

I wasn't a man yet, and even if I was, I wasn't sure I'd be the kind of man who would jump into something without thinking. I liked having a plan and knowing what was going to happen next, but I didn't tell Kendrick that, afraid he'd think I wasn't the right kind of man. Some nights we just sat on the back porch playing checkers, with Kelvin watching quiet as a mouse, and all of us smacking the mosquitos against our arms and legs and then flicking them off, dead as a doornail.

Everything I did with Kendrick was more exciting than anything I did back in Chicago. I wondered if this must be what it felt like to have a brother instead of sisters who sat and talked all day. We even looked a little bit alike. When we all went to the corner store to buy candy, the woman behind the counter told us, "I can tell y'all are family."

"This is my cousin Clem," Kendrick said, pulling my arm like he was proud. On the way home, he showed me all the candy he had shoved in his pocket when the candy store woman wasn't looking. "That's why it's good to go with a crowd," he said, hitting my arm and laughing. There wasn't nothing that scared Kendrick.

Uncle Kent's wife, Aunt Thea, was small and quiet but she smiled pretty and cooked us special things our momma never made, like fried chicken livers with gravy, which I saw

Clarisse spit in her hand, and pineapple upside-down cake. I couldn't get enough of the sweet tea and even though Aunt Thea told me to go easy, I didn't and drank too much and had to climb over arms and legs all night long to get up and go to the bathroom.

Uncle Kent was a lot older than my daddy and had a big stomach and a face full of hair, and I thought they barely looked like brothers.

"Clemson sure spit you out little man," Uncle Kent said to me, rubbing my head.

Clarisse and Annette laughed at that, but I couldn't figure out what was so funny about being spit out, but with everybody laughing and smiling along with Uncle Kent, I smiled too. Annette told me later Uncle Kent just meant that I looked just like our daddy.

"Why didn't he just say that?" I asked her.

"It's just an expression they use down South, Clem," she said, sounding like I was bothering her.

Folks told my momma every Sunday in church, "You have some good-looking children, Cecille." I thought it was maybe because momma always made sure I dressed nice with a jacket and tie and my shoes polished up good. At home, people always said me and my sisters looked just alike, but I sure didn't see how a boy could look like his sisters. And even if everyone thought my sisters were pretty,

I didn't want to look like a girl. But Uncle Kent saying I looked just like my daddy was the first time I'd heard it, and I never knew how good those words could make me could feel. Better even than saying I was as good-looking as my sisters.

ELEVEN

On Sunday we went with Uncle Kent's family to Galilee Baptist Church, and when the pastor asked if there were any visitors, Aunt Thea made the three of us stand and say our names and our church home out loud. After service ended, we went back to the house and changed out of our church clothes, and Uncle Kent took us all out to Lake Park and everybody brought their swimsuits and headed to the water.

"Bet you swim like a fish just like your daddy," Uncle Kent said to me. "Our daddy and granddaddy had us out on the water fishing before we could barely walk."

"Was my daddy good at fishing?" I asked him.

"Pppfffff…" Uncle Kent blew through his lips. "Well, I can't say he was good at fishing. See, fishing was kind of my thang," he said to me, laughing. "I was what they call a natural. Clemson, he was young. And boy he loved to play. Jumping and swimming and acting the fool—till our daddy got in his behind, that is." Uncle Kent laughed again. "But fishing, nah, that was all me."

"So he was good at swimming?" I asked.

"Pppfffff…" Uncle Kent started every sentence with that sound. "Swimming? Now, no one could outswim Clemson.

He left the fish behind." He laughed again. "We always knew he'd head off for the navy or something like that. He was always looking…always looking to help. He was just…good folk…" Uncle Kent looked away, then said softer, "Just good folk." I saw him wipe his face. "Let me get this grill going or we ain't going to eat today," he said, leaving me sitting by the edge of the water. Kendrick tried to drag me in and got Kelvin to help him, but I told him I wasn't feeling good and he finally let go and went back in the water. Next thing, I heard Aunt Thea screaming for him to leave his sisters alone when he was pretending to be a shark and attacking their legs from below.

"He's so tiring," I heard Kara Ann telling Annette when they got out to dry off. I noticed Kendrick never messed with Clarisse, so I knew he had some kind of sense.

When Clarisse and Kandace finally got out, worrying now about their hair getting wet with Kendrick acting the fool, the boys stayed in, and I wished my stomach wasn't bubbling so I could go in and join instead of sitting there on the side being a baby.

K.J. came over and sat next to me. "Hey there, Clemson Junior," he said, pushing me over.

"No one calls me that," I told him.

"They never call you C.J.?" he asked.

"Nope, just Clem." We sat watching Kendrick chase everybody in the water. "He is so crazy," K.J. said, shaking his head.

"You like being a Junior?" I asked him.

He turned to me. "Sure do. It's a big responsibility we got, right? Carrying on our daddies' names." He looked so serious, like the doctor just told him he had one week to live. Like being a Junior was a death sentence.

"How are we supposed to do that?" I asked him.

"Do what?" He was flinging rocks now into the water.

"Carry on our daddies' names. How do you carry on a name?" I asked.

He shrugged. "I don't know. Be like them, I guess. Responsible or whatever," he said, not looking at me.

I flung a few rocks, but they didn't go nearly as far as his.

"Lean back a little and use your whole arm," he said, showing me how he did it.

I tried his way and the rocks went further. "There you go, a little practice and we may just have the next Satchel Paige." He laughed.

"Suppose you don't know what your daddy was like?" I asked him.

"Say what?" he said.

"You said being a Junior means you got to be like your daddy. But suppose you don't know what your daddy was like?" I asked.

"You got me there C.J.," K.J. said. "You got me there."

TWELVE

Aunt Thea walked over. "K.J., go help your daddy with that grill. He's so busy running his mouth he's bound to burn up everything," she said, laughing.

"Yes ma'am," K.J. said, jumping up and wiping the grass off the back of his shorts. He hurried over to Uncle Kent, who I could see from where I was sitting was talking to another family, waving a big fork in his hand with his back to the grill.

"You okay, Clemson?" Aunt Thea asked.

"Yes ma'am, my stomach is hurting a little bit. I'll go in after I eat," I lied.

She patted my knee. "Good, we need you in there to keep an eye on Kendrick." She smiled her pretty smile.

I knew after we ate, everybody would be too tired to go back in the water and I wouldn't need to make up anything else because we'd head on back to the house on Townsend Street.

When two weeks passed, I just about cried my eyes out when it was time to go home. Kendrick didn't cry, though. He waited till I was finished and said, "Clem, if you wasn't my cousin, I'd swear you was a girl with all that crying you doing. Boys ain't supposed to cry like that."

I wiped my face dry. "I can't help it," I told him.

"Sure you can," Kendrick said. "Just think of something else. Something that makes you mad. That stops the crying every time."

I was thinking Kendrick could probably write a book about the rules for what boys can and can't do.

K.J. put all of our suitcases in the trunk of the car and opened the back door of Uncle Kent's car. "Ready to go," he said, smiling. He went and sat in the driver's seat like he was our personal chauffeur. Kendrick said K.J. just got his license and he drove now more than Uncle Kent. If you took away the belly and the face full of hair, K.J. was like a younger version of my uncle. I guess just like a Junior was supposed to be.

"Don't go nowhere yet," Kendrick said, and ran back into the house.

By the time he came back out, we were getting into the backseat to head off to the train station where Momma was going to meet us to take us home. He poked his head in through the open window and told me, "Close your eyes and open your hand." I felt something cold and hard drop in my palm, and I opened my eyes to see Kendrick's pocketknife.

"You can have it," he told me. I'd played with it the whole time we were in Milwaukee because Momma never let me have one. She told me I was too young, and I would hurt myself. She didn't care if other boys had them, "Knives are dangerous," she told me. But I found out, that's what made them fun. Me and Kendrick used his knife to dig up ant tunnels, worked on our aim by throwing it at a bull's-eye we drew in chalk on a tree, and whittled sticks into spears we had to hide from Aunt Thea because that would mean we really were going to hurt someone or get hurt. And then we chased each other, but mainly Kelvin, till he ran and hid.

"I can't," I told him. Looking down at that pretty bone handle that Kendrick had burned with a flame, then carved his initials, *K.T.*, into.

"I'll just get me another one," he said, winking at me.

I had no idea what that meant, but I knew that somehow, Kendrick would find a way to get himself another knife. "I'll get the same one again, and we'll each have one," he told me. "But you gotta put your initials on it too," he added, pointing below his. "Right here, *K.T.* and *C.T.*"

I nodded and put it in my pocket before he changed his mind.

Clarisse and Annette were out the other window hugging Kandace and Kara Ann and Aunt Thea.

"Y'all ready?" Uncle Kent asked. I shook my head, but I thought I'd never be ready to leave Kendrick behind.

Uncle Kent took a new job, Momma told us, driving a truck, and he's gone most of the week, so we couldn't go right back to Milwaukee. Momma said she's thinking about sending for our cousins soon to come visit in Chicago. I think Kendrick could even turn Chicago upside down.

Uncle Kent told us that even though there were just the two of them, he and my daddy lived near all their cousins growing up in South Carolina and it felt like they had a whole family of brothers and sisters. I wished then my daddy was still living, and we could move to Milwaukee, right next door to Uncle Kent and his family. I knew I'd miss Chicago, but I couldn't imagine anything better than living near family and feeling like I had a whole houseful of brothers and sisters even when I didn't.

THIRTEEN

I'd forgotten how happy Momma could be but then I saw her face at the Everett Street train station in Milwaukee. She was standing there on the platform when Annette shouted, "Momma!" And Momma came running, just about knocking us down. She hugged us all tight at once, wet kissing.

She kissed and hugged Uncle Kent too and told K.J. how big and handsome he was. After we said our goodbyes and the four us were alone, she grabbed us again just like she did when we left weeks earlier. Clarisse stepped back, staring at momma's uniform, her face wrinkled up like she smelled something bad.

"I didn't even have time to change," Momma said to us, but really to Clarisse. She smoothed down the front of her uniform like it had wrinkles and fixed her collar. "Mrs. You-know-who kept me so late I almost missed the train." Clarisse turned her head away.

Momma pulled us all in close again. "Momma, can this wait till we get home?" Clarisse said, looking around.

Momma laughed. "Well, I'm sorry if I've missed you all so much," she said, but she finally stopped with all the kissing. On the short train ride back to Chicago, I told Momma every single thing we did in Milwaukee, leaving out some of the craziest things I saw Kendrick do. As soon as we got home, Momma had us unpack our things while she started on supper—fried chicken with okra and the biscuits I love. And she had just taken the chocolate cake out of the oven when we heard the fireworks.

"What was that?" Annette asked, running to the window in the front room. Clarisse followed behind her and yelled to the kitchen, "Come look at all the people out here."

Me and Momma ran to the other window, and people were outside all up and down the street like the block parties they sometimes had on South Parkway.

"Let's go see what's going on," Clarisse said, kicking off her slippers and looking for her shoes.

The four of us ran down to the front stoop and by the time we got there, the street looked even more crowded, with people out front and hanging out windows. There was music playing and car horns honking, and folks were kissing and whooping and hollering like I'd never heard before.

"Our boys are coming home!" a woman yelled from an apartment window across the street.

"Wha—" Momma looked around. "The war's over?"

We all turned to look at Momma. She looked up at the sky, like she was asking the stars and the moon, and in the dark with the fireworks flashing above, we could see the tears running down her cheeks.

"Let's go upstairs," Annette said to me and Clarisse, looking scared.

I took Momma's hand, but she wouldn't move. "The war's over," she said again. Not asking this time but saying it loud and clear.

"Hallelujah! Sure is!" a man said behind us, clapping his hands. He continued on down the street past our stoop.

"Momma, let's go on up," Annette said, trying to grab her other hand.

Momma half fell, half sat on the steps. "Help me, Clarisse," Annette said.

The two of them tried to lift Momma under her arms. I tried too, but all of a sudden, she seemed like she weighed about one thousand pounds.

"Y'all need some help here?"

I looked up and it was Errol's father, Mr. Watkins. When he leaned over all I could smell was the drink on his breath, like he'd started celebrating early.

"No, we'll be fine," Clarisse said, cold, like she wasn't speaking to an adult. But even with all he had to drink, he could see we needed help. He stumbled a bit but pulled Momma up with one arm and got her to her feet.

I stepped forward. "Thank you, Mr. Watkins, we'll be fine from here."

Momma looked in his eyes, not saying a word, and started walking on her own, up the stairs to our apartment.

"You're welcome!" I heard Mr. Watkins yell to her back, his words slurred. Momma stopped and stood a little straighter but didn't turn around, just kept on walking.

I sure hoped Mr. Watkins wasn't going up to the apartment to start up something with Errol's mother, because Momma wouldn't be able to sit and talk about Mrs. Watkins's problems with her husband tonight. Instead, we were gonna do our best to get her into bed and do for Momma what she did for Mrs. Watkins. And then we would have to turn up the radio to quiet the sounds of the party outside, and hope and pray that while everyone else was celebrating on the South Side, our momma would fall asleep to one of us rubbing her back, listening to the music of the Ink Spots, and not have too much time to think about the husband she'd never get the chance to welcome home.

FOURTEEN

Since Errol started at Lincoln, as far as anyone could tell, we were friends. Wasn't my job to tell them anything different. And seeing as there wasn't a long line of folks waiting to be friends with the Professor, and Errol was the new kid last year who didn't know anyone, it worked out just fine. I don't know how Errol did in his other school and since he wasn't talking, I'll guess I'll never know, but here at Lincoln, as long as Errol stayed quiet in the back of the class and minded his own business, he'd do all right.

I thought being the Professor and helping out with answers made me safe from what some of the other boys had to deal with. The fighting and being pushed around and teased all the time. As far as I could tell, near everybody in class liked me. But what made sixth grade different from fifth grade was that I learned that there's two kinds of smart. I had one kind of smart, and Curtis Whittaker was about to teach me another.

I stayed clear of Curtis since he started at Lincoln two years ago. When you get boys like Curtis, who don't give two licks about spelling tests or homework, being a little professor ain't no help at all.

Curtis ran the school yard like he was a general. Two times bigger than anyone else and every day acting like he was leading troops into battle. Me, Errol, and anybody else who got in his way was the enemy. His body was the tank.

My daddy might have been a soldier, fighting against the Japanese, but every day, I was just trying to survive Curtis and his troops.

Once Curtis realized I was too small for his army, not good enough at stickball, and too smart to sit in the back of the classroom, he didn't have no use for me at all.

And when you got problems with Curtis, you got problems.

Now if Curtis was just a little bit smarter, he might have noticed me long before we hit sixth grade, but Curtis Whittaker ain't known for being quick. But once I did catch his eye, Curtis made up for lost time.

The first time, I got off easy when Curtis just shoved me down in the school yard as school let out and all I got was a busted lip.

Errol looked at me, laughing.

But the next day, when Curtis did the same to Errol, he wasn't smiling then.

"I see you ain't laughing today," I told Errol, giving

him the same smile he gave me the day before. Errol looked mad.

"We ain't got a chance against Curtis," he said to me, wiping his lip.

"That's about the smartest thing I ever heard you say," I told him.

Me and Errol ain't alike in nearly anything, but neither one of us wanted anything to do with trying to fight Curtis.

Me and Errol took to walking fast after school, hoping Curtis wouldn't catch us. When Curtis found out, he had one of his troops wait at the front door early. When we took our time, Curtis was as patient as could be, sitting with his buddies on the front steps of the school, legs stretched out long. "What took y'all so long?" he'd say when we finally came downstairs after hiding out in the stairwell for what seemed like hours.

"Thanks for waiting," I said, "I was scared to walk home by myself." But Curtis liked jokes even less than he liked me and Errol.

"Stop messing with him," Errol told me, like it was my fault I got hit in the head.

"You got any better ideas, you let me know," I said, holding my head where Curtis had smacked me so hard, he left a mark.

"Maybe Annette and Clarisse could meet you after school," Momma told me that night when she got home from work and saw my lip.

"I can't have my sisters walk me home, Momma!"

"For the life of me, I do not understand what is wrong with these boys," Momma said, pressing too hard on my lips with a cloth smelling of the red stuff she puts on when we get a cut.

"Ow, Momma!" I said, turning away. "I'll be fine."

"This does not look like fine to me. Where was Errol? I told you, the two of you need to stick together."

"Me and Errol ain't exactly Al Capone's gang. We're not gonna scare anybody away."

"We'll have to think of something," Momma said, looking worried.

The next day, when Curtis grabbed me from behind and ripped my shirt, Clarisse and Annette gave me their two cents.

"You gonna have to learn to fight back," Annette said. "Momma told Mrs. Watkins she's gonna go speak to the principal if it keeps up."

"And. You. Don't. Want. That," Clarisse said, poking me in my arm with each word.

One sure way to get a beating worse than you got is to have your momma tell the principal on the boy who beat you.

"I can't do nothing to Curtis," I said to Annette. "He's bigger than Clarisse."

"You want another fat lip, Clem?" Clarisse asked me.

"You're gonna at least have to stand up for yourself. Even if you lose," Annette told me.

"How's the Cowardly Lion from *The Wizard of Oz* going to stick up for himself?" Clarisse laughed. "You want *me* to go take care of him?"

That sounded like a good idea to me, but I kept that to myself.

"Don't tell Momma about my shirt," I said to Annette.

"What are you gonna tell her then, *I* ripped it?" Clarisse asked.

Me and Annette looked at each other.

"Can I?" I asked.

"And then I get in trouble? Nuh-uh," Clarisse said, shaking her head back and forth so hard her big curls swung in her eyes.

"I'll tell Momma it was an accident," Annette said.

"Momma always believes Annette," I added.

And all of a sudden Clarisse's head stopped shaking. "And what do I get?"

"What do you want?" I asked.

"I'll let you know," Clarisse said to me, smiling just as sweet as could be.

I was about to learn quick, probably the only thing worse than getting beat up at school, and then maybe having your momma tell the principal on the boy who beat you up at school, was seeing Clarisse smile that big Silver Streak Pontiac smile and knowing I was about to owe her a favor.

FIFTEEN

Every Thursday I lied to Errol and told him I had to go and help my momma at her job. Thank the Lord Curtis was too dumb to figure out my secret back door escape route. And thank the Lord Errol didn't ask questions either, because even someone with half a brain would know that me going to help my momma at her job didn't make any kind of sense. First off, the Franklins hired Cecille Thurber to dust and mop their floors and cook their meals, not her son. And second, my momma would rather throw herself in front of the el train before she let any one of her children work as a maid.

On Thursdays, after I lied to Errol and snuck out of the back of the school instead of the front toward our apartment building, I turned left and walked down a long, pretty street till I got to Michigan Avenue and the George Cleveland Hall Branch library.

My momma's been taking me, Annette, and Clarisse to the library for as long as I can remember. A few years back, Momma started letting me go on my own some Saturdays once my chores were done and only, she said, if I went "right there and back." Thank goodness she didn't mention Errol's name. Momma ain't no dummy. She knows the last thing

Errol Watkins wants to do is go to the library. Sometimes Momma used to ask me to pick up something for her at the library too. "You know what I like, Clem," she'd say. And I do. It's gotta be one of those mystery books where somebody kills somebody for their money on the first page and the writer tries to make you think it's anybody except who you think it is, only to find out on the very last page it was the person you thought it was from the very beginning.

I don't have time for those kinds of books.

With her job at the Franklins, Momma didn't have time to read like she used to, but when I went, I still picked out a book now and then for her and left it next to the couch. But I could tell it hadn't moved from the spot I put it in by the time I needed to return it.

Most of my time at the library was spent downstairs. The librarian there was Miss Cook and sometimes I thought, after my momma, she was about the nicest person I ever met.

"How's your family, Clem?" she asked me almost every time I saw her. And since my daddy died, it's like she made it her job to be my very own personal librarian.

At first, of course Clarisse and Annette came with us too, staying in the section with bigger books and longer chapters. I could always hear Clarisse's loud whispering no matter how many times Miss Cook or the other librarians put their fingers to their lips. By the time we left, we all had a stack of books to check out, and at home, we'd show each other what we got. Up until Daddy died, Momma always picked one book she could read aloud to all of us at night, and there wasn't nothing I loved more than hearing her voice, strong but still soft too, acting out every part in the book. I liked to sit right up close to her and sometimes lay my head on her arm so I could feel her body move as she turned the pages.

It was Momma who told Miss Cook how much I loved maps. And the next time I showed up downstairs, Miss Cook had books waiting just for me that made me realize there was a whole lot of world to see outside of Chicago, Illinois.

"You might like this one, Clem," she said to me one day when I showed up, handing me a book called *Five on a Treasure Island,* about a boy who goes on adventures with his sisters and cousins all over the world. On the cover was a small white boy standing in the middle of a boat.

Now when I read those books, they make me wish it was me and Kendrick and all of my Milwaukee cousins.

"Do they get lost?" I asked Miss Cook.

"You'll have to tell me," she said, sweet as could be.

So I finished extra quick so I could get back to the library and tell Miss Cook exactly what happened to everyone in the book. She looked like I was telling her the most interesting story in the world. And then after I finished my telling, she gave me another one about another adventure she'd been keeping at the desk just for me.

"There's another one?" I asked her. "With the same people?"

"Yes, Clem." She laughed. "It's a series, so you can read as many as you like."

I read that one too, but not as fast as the first. Because sitting at home reading these books was like making new friends and traveling with them all over the world without ever leaving Chicago.

SIXTEEN

Me and Errol first saw him on the playground at recess.

"Who's that?" I pointed across the school yard. Of course, Errol didn't notice a thing. But before we could find out, I saw Curtis walk over and introduce himself to the new boy. I'm sure it wasn't a "How do you do, welcome to Lincoln Elementary," but when I saw Curtis puffing up his chest and standing tall, I knew he was making sure that new boy knew who was running things. Funny thing is, the new boy didn't look scared. He didn't look no kind of way, really. He stood looking at Curtis like he didn't care much about what he said.

Once Curtis moved out of sight, I hit Errol in the arm.

"Let's go see what's up," I told him.

"For what?" he asked.

I swear, there were days I just knew God had a seat waiting in heaven for making me have to deal with Errol every day.

We came up behind the new boy. He was smaller than I thought, closer to my size than Errol's.

"You the new one, right?" I asked him.

"Yup," he said. "Lymon." No more than that.

Please God, I thought to myself. *Not two Errols.*

I tried again.

"You best not mess with Curtis," I warned him.

"Who, Fat Boy?" He laughed. "He don't scare me."

There was something about his laugh, and his eyes, one a little smaller than the other, made me laugh right along with him. I stepped in closer. Me and Errol introduced ourselves. When Lymon told me he was from Milwaukee, I couldn't get the words out fast enough trying to figure if he knew Uncle Kent, Aunt Thea, and of course, Kendrick. By the time I ran down everybody's name and realized he didn't know not one, I was just about out of breath. The whole time I was talking, he was smiling at me, with those squinty little eyes. Errol stood there watching, not saying much as usual. When the school bell rang, the three of us walked back in together. I had a lot more questions for this new boy, but I figured I asked enough for one day. I thought then about my sister Annette and how sometimes maybe the best way to get the answers you want is to keep quiet, listen, and watch.

Lymon Caldwell might have been from Milwaukee, but he sure loved Chicago like he was born here. Lymon asked if he could walk with us home from school since he lived a few blocks over on St. Lawrence, and when he walked, he still looked around like it was Christmas morning. He'd look in the doorways of every pool hall and stop dead in the street if someone walked by in a fancy suit.

"Close your mouth, you're letting flies in," I told him, laughing at the way his mouth hung open wide when he saw something he liked.

"What's that over there?" he asked, pointing at a building on the corner.

"Forum Hall," I told him. "It's a jazz club. You know—scoot dee doo, scat doo watt…"

He laughed. "Fool, you don't know nothing 'bout no jazz."

"Tell me I didn't sound like Pops himself," I said. I made my voice low as I could and started scatting again in my Louis Armstrong voice.

"Me, I got music in my blood," Lymon told us.

"How's that?" Errol asked.

Now it was my turn for my mouth to hang open. *Errol was asking questions?*

"Back in Mississippi—"

"Mississippi? I thought you said you was from Milwaukee?" Errol asked his second question of the day.

"So you're a country Negro?" I laughed.

Lymon stopped and his eyes got smaller. "Who you calling country? I didn't say Mississippi. I said Milwaukee. You can't hear?"

I looked at Errol, and Errol looked at the ground.

I put my finger in my ear. "Maybe I got a little wax in my ears," I said, laughing.

"Maybe you need to clean 'em out," Lymon said, and smiled a little. We kept right on walking.

Seemed like overnight it went from me and Errol to the Three Musketeers. With me talking all the time and Errol hardly at all, Lymon fit right in between. I was the only one with sisters. Lymon had two little brothers he called Bad and Badder, and Errol didn't say much about being home all by himself, but together, all hating on Curtis Whittaker, we made out fine.

"Why don't you sit in back with us?" Lymon asked one day at lunch when we were going down the list again of the most beautiful women, starting with Miss Lena Horne.

"I can't see too good," I told him. "I need to sit close to the board." Errol looked up from his sandwich, like he was about to say something.

"Last thing the Professor needs is glasses too," I said, laughing.

After Curtis made his introduction to Lymon, and Lymon didn't look like Curtis made any difference to him one way or another, I told Lymon, "You better watch your back with Curtis."

Much as I loved being the Three Musketeers, with finally someone who said more than two words a day, what I loved most about being a threesome with Lymon was that it kept Curtis away. I think he was watching Lymon just as close as

I was, not sure yet what to make of him. Something about Lymon seemed familiar to me, but I couldn't quite put my finger on it.

"Yeah? What's Curtis gonna do to me?" Lymon asked.

Errol just shook his head. "You seen what he does. He start in on you, he ain't never gonna stop."

"He start in on the two of you?" Lymon asked us. We didn't say nothing.

"And you didn't fight back?" He looked surprised and mad at the same time.

"You sound like my sisters," I told him. "What do we look like tryin' to fight Curtis Whittaker? He's big enough to be somebody's daddy."

Lymon laughed out loud then.

"The bigger they are, the harder they fall." Lymon looked like he meant it.

And Errol looked impressed. "Sounds like you got a plan."

"A plan to get killed," I told them both.

I couldn't tell if Lymon Caldwell was scared, stupid, or brave. Didn't take long before I found out that he was just maybe all three at once.

SEVENTEEN

Wasn't none of us expecting for it to happen the way it did. Especially not Curtis. The three of us had gotten used to not having to worry about Curtis anymore out at recess or after school. We sat over in the corner of the school yard, where it was quiet and out of sight. Sometimes Errol brought cards for us to play, but today he and Lymon stood listening to me tell them about Clarisse and how we had another fight that Annette had to break up. I added in all kinds of good lines I got in about Clarisse's face and the pimples she sometimes got. Of course, Errol was all ears, because wasn't no one more interested in hearing stories about Clarisse than Errol, but I could tell Lymon was only half listening. Just as I was acting out the part where Clarisse came running after me, I looked up to see Curtis standing right behind Lymon. I didn't have time to warn him, but when I stopped talking and Lymon looked in my face, he knew right away who I was looking at. He didn't turn. Just stood still waiting.

"Le-mon," Curtis said, leaning into Lymon, like they were going steady and he was whispering sweet nothings in his ear.

Errol tried to pull Lymon away, but he didn't move. Now

our quiet corner was starting to get crowded with everyone coming over to see what was going to happen.

"Go on and hit him, Curtis," I heard one of his army tell him, and I knew Lymon was in trouble then.

Lymon finally turned around and stood facing Curtis. He shoved Lymon hard in the chest, but Lymon didn't go down. I stepped closer to see for myself why Lymon wasn't backing away.

"Hurry, teacher's coming!" a boy named Russell yelled. And by the time we all looked over to where he was pointing, Lymon had swung on Curtis so hard, he nearly broke his nose. Blood went flying everywhere. One of the girls screamed.

"He got him!" I yelled, not really believing what I just saw.

Lymon and Curtis stood face-to-face, breathing hard and staring each other down. Blood was dripping from Curtis's nose. And we all just stood quiet watching to see Curtis's next move, but he didn't have one. Now I remembered why Lymon seemed so familiar. Not since Kendrick had I met someone who didn't let anything scare him.

By the time the teacher got to them and snatched them both up, everybody knew it was Lymon who was in charge now. And with me and Errol, his two new best friends, I guess that meant we were in charge too.

We stayed the Three Musketeers, but with Lymon and Errol in the back of the class and me in the front, it felt more like Three Musketeers minus one. Sometimes I'd turn to see the two of them sitting in the back of the classroom, Errol laughing good over his shoulder at something Lymon said. All of a sudden, the Errol I thought I knew, the Errol who could barely spell the word *joke,* was laughing at everything Lymon said. I thought Lymon was funny and all, but he wasn't no Eddie Rochester. Since Lymon's fight with Curtis, we stuck closer to him, but just about everybody else steered clear.

"They think I got the plague or something?" Lymon once asked at lunch, when we three were sitting all alone.

"Nah," Errol told him. "They just scared of you is all."

"Because of Curtis?" he asked.

I sat listening and wondering how it would feel to have everyone in school afraid of you. But Lymon seemed like it wasn't what he wanted at all. I sat watching him eating his sandwich like he didn't have a care in the world. Not afraid of anyone or anything.

He looked up at me. "You gonna eat your lunch or ask me to go steady?" Errol laughed loud.

I smiled. "I heard you and Curtis were already dating." I held my breath and waited until he smiled back.

There were days I couldn't tell what Lymon was thinking.

One day he'd laugh all day long and the next he'd look like a pot about to boil over.

"I see you took my advice," Annette said to me one day after the fight with Curtis and Lymon in the school yard.

"Huh?" I asked her, working on my schoolwork.

"My advice? About standing up for yourself."

"Why do you say that?" I asked her.

"Well, let's see." She held up one finger, "No more busted lips." Then she held up a second finger, "No more black eyes," and a third, "No more—" I stopped her.

"That ain't me. It's Lymon, the new kid me and Errol are friends with."

"Lymon? Kind of name is Lymon?" she asked, digging through the icebox.

"He just moved here from Milwaukee. Curtis is scared of him."

"So he's bigger than Curtis?"

"Not bigger, he just put Curtis in his place."

"So what you're saying is, he stands up for himself," she said, staring at me with her hand on her hip.

"Not now, Annette," I told her.

"But I was right, wasn't I?" Annette bit into her apple. And I kept looking at my paper.

"So, you like this Lymon?" she asked me, nicer now.

I looked up at her. "I think so. I—"

"What?"

"Never mind. Yeah, I like him. Curtis doesn't even look at me anymore."

"Well, you showed Curtis, didn't you?" Annette said as she turned to leave. "The way you're going, you're gonna earn a Purple Heart in no time." I could hear her laughing all the way to her room.

Lymon Caldwell might have saved me from Curtis, but he could never save me from my sisters.

The truth was that for the rest of sixth grade, being safe from Curtis wasn't the best part about having Lymon around. The times with Errol, like lunch and recess and walking home from school, Lymon made better, just by being in between the two of us. He made Errol talk more and that meant I could talk less. And somehow it all just worked together.

EIGHTEEN

The night before my last day of sixth grade at Lincoln Elementary, Momma opened the front door in a hurry, holding a paper sack. "I got a surprise for you," she told me when I went to give her a hug. She was smiling big, and I was hoping the Franklins had some of their fancy dinner company over and Momma had brought home a piece of one of their pretty desserts. Maybe the lemon cake with the sugary frosting and the raspberry filling in the middle. But it wasn't no dessert, I could tell by how big the bag was.

Clarisse and Annette were at the kitchen table, and they were supposed to be doing homework. But I could hear them whispering so I knew that meant I couldn't go nowhere near the kitchen because they were talking about girl things, which really meant boy things, and I wasn't in the mood to hear any of that. Like I always did, I made a big deal about Momma being home, so they would know and cut out the whispering and get back to their schoolwork before Momma came in the kitchen. But this night Momma wasn't her usual tired self. I wasn't sure Clarisse and Annette heard Momma come in, so I was talking extra loud hoping they'd cut out the whispering.

"So I just open it up right now?" I asked her.

"Lower your voice, Clem. And yes, open it now." Momma nodded, smiling.

I dug down deep in the bottom and pulled out a pair of slippery tan shorts with a wide white belt at the waist.

"Shorts? Thanks, Momma," I said, wondering why Momma thought this was a special surprise. I already had about four pairs plus one pair of dungarees, and I knew with Momma not buying any more clothes now, it took a lot for her to buy me these.

Last Saturday, before Momma went off to her Saturday shift, and before Clarisse and Annette woke up, I heard her talking to Dr. Stanford out in the hallway.

"Mrs. Thurber, I think we can both agree I have been very patient," he said to Momma, but he didn't sound like he was being patient. He sounded mad.

"Yes…very patient…husband…more time." Momma's voice kept going in and out, maybe because she was crying, maybe because she was trying hard to make sure we couldn't hear any of the conversation in the apartment. But whatever she was doing to keep things quiet, Dr. Stanford didn't seem to notice.

He spoke a little louder. "I understand your circumstances, and while I respect the sacrifice of your husband, I cannot continue to overlook the fact that you are a month behind on your rent. I will give you two weeks, Mrs. Thurber. Two weeks to have my rent. If at that time you are unable to come up with the money, I will have no choice but to ask you to move on." Sounded like now it was Momma who was asking for a rain check and it was Dr. Sanford who was saying no.

Momma went on down the steps after Dr. Sanford left, off to the Franklins', and I went into the kitchen to eat breakfast. When I finished, I sat quiet waiting.

Annette walked in an hour later, rubbing her eyes, and jumped when she saw me sitting there.

"Are we going to have to move?" I asked her.

"Clem, it's too early," she said to me, putting water on the stove for tea.

But when I didn't say anything else, Annette looked over at me. I could feel the tears starting, but I kept the thought of Dr. Stanford's mean voice and Momma's crying in my head to make me mad, and that held them back.

"Momma can't pay the rent," I said, not sure if I was asking Annette or telling her. Even though the tears didn't come, I could still hear the shakiness in my voice. Annette pretended she didn't notice and sat down across from me.

"I don't think we're going to have to move," she said.

"You don't *think* so?" I almost yelled.

"Lower your voice, Clem," she said. "You want Clarisse in here?" I shook my head.

"Momma got a little bit behind is all. But, you know, things have been tough since Daddy passed. She'll most likely have to do what she always does."

"What does she always do?" I asked.

Annette breathed in deep. "She asks her sisters for help. She doesn't like doing it, but Aunt Dorcas and Aunt Bethel send her money from time to time when things get tough. They know Momma's got a lot on her plate."

"A lot on her plate like the three of us?" I asked.

"Like the three of us," Annette said. "We all gotta make sacrifices is all. But she'll get caught up."

I nodded. "But why didn't anybody just tell me that?"

"Maybe you just weren't listening." The kettle started whistling and Annette stood up again.

NINETEEN

"Those aren't just any shorts, Clem. They are swim shorts."
Momma was going on about the shorts and I hadn't seen her
look this happy in so long, it was making me happy too.

"Swim shorts?" I didn't understand.

"Sit down," Momma told me. She fell back on the couch,
taking off her clunky work shoes.

"Hi, Momma." Clarisse and Annette came in. Annette
kissed Momma on the cheek. Clarisse just smiled.

"Show them what I just brought you, Clem," Momma
told me.

I held up my swim trunks.

"Oooh yay, Clem is going to drown," Clarisse said,
laughing.

"Not with swim lessons he's not," Momma said, proud.

"Clem's getting swim lessons?" Annette sat down next
to Momma.

I don't think we'd ever heard of anyone colored getting
swim lessons before. Out at the beach on Lake Michigan,
folks went and splashed around. Some swam, but far as we
knew, nobody was giving out lessons. Either you knew how
to swim or you didn't. Those who didn't stayed close to the

edge. Those who did swam out far. If you didn't and were stupid enough to swim out far, you drowned. Simple as that.

There's nothing Momma loves more than telling a story, so the next thing I knew, Momma sat way back in the cushions and started in.

"You know how Mrs. Franklin is always in my business? 'Does Clarisse have a boyfriend yet? And isn't Clem going into fifth grade this year?' She nearly had a fit when I told her he skipped a grade." Momma stopped to laugh. "Skipped a grade?" she said in her Mrs. Franklin voice, high and squeaky, with the fingers of her hand spread out across her chest like she was about to faint. "'Why, that must mean he's *very* smart.' Do you know she had the nerve to ask me where he got his intelligence from?" Clarisse stopped her.

"Momma, you know you told us this before, right?"

"Shut up, Clarisse, and let Momma tell the story the way she wants to tell it," I said.

"Oh, that's because it's about you being so smart—"

"Can we please hear the story?" Annette said.

"Well, this morning, Mrs. Franklin came into the kitchen while I was preparing lunch. And she said, 'CeeCee, would you mind making a couple of extra sandwiches for this afternoon? Matthew will be heading over to the club pool today. He has swim lessons this week before he heads off to camp and I'll need you to pack extra sandwiches for his instructor.' Now you know the last thing I want to do is have any kind of conversation with Mrs. Franklin, so at first I said, 'Sure thing, Mrs. Franklin. I hope he likes tuna fish.' And then I thought about Clem wanting to learn to swim." Momma looked at me with wet eyes. "And I thought, God gave you a mouth, and Cecille Thurber, you better go on ahead and use it. So, just as she was about to leave the kitchen, I said, 'Excuse me, Mrs. Franklin. How much do those swim lessons cost? Because since my Clemson died serving this country, all my Clem can talk about is learning how to swim.' I think she was so shocked, she said yes to the lessons before she had a chance to think about it. Even offered to pay. Of course, she'll get it out of me one way or the other with her 'Do you think you could come in just a little bit early tomorrow morning because Mr. Franklin one thing or the other,' but—"

"So Clem is going to a white folks' pool with their son Matthew to get lessons?" Clarisse interrupted Momma again.

"Yes," Momma said, looking straight at me. "It's before the pool opens, Mrs. Franklin said. The swim teacher offers private lessons at a pool in a building over on Fiftieth Street. She'll need to get permission from the building owner. Of course, with Mr. Franklin being who he is, that won't be a problem. No one will make much of a fuss about one colored boy getting lessons as long as he's their guest, and no one has to see him, of course, that early in the morning. It being a private lesson and all. And as long as he's with Matthew. She made it clear that this was a *very special circumstance*. A *huge favor* to me. For the *sacrifice* of my husband and all." Momma's eyes rolled as she stretched out all the words Mrs. Franklin had used so that she never had to actually say out loud that *Colored Folks and White Folks Should Never Be Sharing Swimming Pools.*

"Well then, can I go too? I don't know how to swim either," Clarisse said.

"Clarisse, I have never heard you say one thing about wanting to learn to swim."

"You never asked me."

"Clarisse, all you want to do is lay out in a bathing suit while the boys watch." Annette laughed.

"I can't help what the boys do." Clarisse winked at her.

"Enough of that!" Momma said, serious. "You girls finish your schoolwork?"

They nodded their heads.

"Clem, you already missed one lesson, and tomorrow is the last day of school, but on Wednesday morning you are going to get up with me and go to your first lesson. You're smart, you'll catch on fast." Momma hugged me tight.

"I told you I'd figure something out," she whispered in my ear.

TWENTY

Usually the first day of school and the last day of school are the best days of the year. And even though we'd never be coming back to Lincoln Elementary and would be going off to Haines Junior High School blocks away in September, I couldn't make myself get excited.

"You leaving tomorrow?" I asked Errol.

"Yup," Errol said. "My dad's driving me first thing."

"You go to North Carolina every summer?" Lymon asked him.

"Yeah, my grandmother's there and some of my cousins too. It ain't too bad, but God dawg my nana makes me get up early! She don't believe in summer vacation."

We laughed. Since Lymon came, Errol went and found himself a sense of humor.

"You going to visit your aunts?" he asked me next.

I looked up at the sky and held my hands together. "Thank the sweet Lord Jesus, not until July. If I survive, I'll see you all in seventh grade." I laughed.

I told Errol and Lymon all about my aunts in D.C. and how me Annette and Clarisse took the train to visit them every summer. I told them about the museum visits and their parlor and fancy ways. But I never told them about the swim lessons I was going to take with Matthew Franklin.

"Wish I had somewhere to go," Lymon said, quiet.

Lymon sometimes told us about his crazy little brothers, but not much about his momma and her new husband. I know enough to know that sometimes not saying anything is saying plenty. There were days he came to school looking so beat-up, you'd think he'd gone a few rounds with Sugar Ray Robinson before breakfast. Once when his eye was puffy and red, I asked him, "Your eye gonna be all right? It looks—" and Lymon turned on me so fast I nearly wet my pants.

"So you a professor *and* a nurse?" he snapped. I noticed he didn't call me a doctor like a man, but a nurse, like a girl.

"Nope." I smiled. "Just a professor."

I knew I shouldn't have bothered, but the next morning, on the way to school, I tried to talk to Errol.

"What do you think is going on with Lymon?" I asked him.

"Ain't my business," Errol said, just like I thought he would.

"I didn't say it was your business. I asked what do you think is going on?"

He walked quiet for a bit. "You so smart and you acting like you don't know?" he said.

And that was the last time me and Errol talked about Lymon.

On the days Lymon came to school looking like he was beat-up on the outside and the inside, we stuck by him. And even though we were friends, the Three Musketeers, I realized most days I felt like everybody else in school. Scared of him.

TWENTY-ONE

After my daddy died was when I decided I wanted to learn to swim. When Daddy was in the navy, Momma told me Daddy was the best swimmer she ever saw. "Like he was born in water," she said her eyes looking all dreamy.

"I want to learn to swim," I told her, hoping my momma would be proud of me the way she was of my daddy.

"I'll have to see about that, Clem," Momma said. "There aren't many places here in Chicago for colored to get lessons, but let me see what I can find."

"Where did Daddy learn?" I asked her.

"Oh, your daddy learned when he was younger than you, down in Ashley River. Said his big brother threw him in and it was either swim or drown, so he started swimming and never stopped." Momma laughed. "When he enlisted in the navy, he was one of the only colored men they didn't have to teach to swim to pass the test."

"Do you know how to swim?" I asked her.

"Never been interested. I don't mind splashing around a bit, but swimming? In a pool? No thank you." She smiled at me. "But you are going to be a swimmer just like your daddy."

"And then I'm going to join the navy and travel all over the world," I told Momma.

Momma shook her head. "Yes, Clemson Junior. Just like your daddy."

Me and Matthew Franklin's teacher was a man with white hair, wearing a one-piece swimsuit I thought only girls wore. He had a big cross in the middle of his suit and small writing underneath that spelled out RED CROSS.

"My name is Mr. Hotchkiss, and I will be your swim instructor." He reached out to shake my hand. "Our Matthew here is off to a good start and I am sure you will catch up to him quickly if you pay close attention." Mr. Hotchkiss sounded like he was training us to be in the military. I stood up straighter.

I might have been the smallest one in my class, but with Matthew Franklin I was at least a head taller. Of course, he was only in second grade at a school I never even heard of. My momma said he wasn't any trouble at all, quiet as a mouse, and if she didn't know any better, she'd swear Mrs. Franklin wasn't his natural momma, he was so sweet.

I looked around the pool and noticed it was so early, it was mostly empty. There were some old people swimming back and forth in swim caps, and they made swimming look as easy as breathing. I wondered how long it would take before I could swim like that.

"Young man." Mr. Hotchkiss was looking at me. "You will need to pay attention to the safety instructions before we begin your lessons."

I nodded but went back to looking around. The pool was small but off to the side was an even smaller baby pool connected to the big pool. I thought if we had a baby pool like this in our neighborhood, or even a pool at all, and I went there every day when I was younger, I wouldn't need these lessons now.

Mr. Hotchkiss had us step down a ladder and into the pool at the shallow end. The water was so cold I bit down on my tongue. I took my time getting in.

Matthew was already in the water, up to his chest, waiting.

"Don't worry," Mr. Hotchkiss said. "You'll warm up in the water." I looked down from the ladder. The water was a pretty, shimmery blue and I could see clear to the bottom, where I could read 2 FT painted in white. I couldn't remember how tall I was. I knew I was taller than Matthew and knew I had to be taller than two feet, but from here, with the water rippling, it looked as deep as the ocean.

I closed my eyes thinking about the bravest things I'd ever had to do—survive losing my daddy, watch my momma lose my daddy, skip from third grade to fourth, survive Curtis Whittaker. And when that didn't work, I thought of the bravest people I knew—Clarisse, Kendrick, Lymon, and my daddy. I tried as hard as I could to remember my daddy's face from his pictures, and think about how scared he must have been in the navy, loading explosives onto ships every day, knowing only colored soldiers got the jobs that could get them blown up, but he did it anyhow until he did get blown up. I stepped down off the ladder into the pool and the water was barely at my waist.

"There we go," Mr. Hotchkiss said. "Now, let's get started."

Looking out at all the water in front of me made me think of my daddy, blown apart, somewhere in the bottom of the Pacific Ocean. Knowing how to swim didn't help him in the end. Cold as I was when I got in the water, my body was on fire now.

"I have to go to the bathroom," I told the teacher.

"Hurry up then," he told me, looking only at Matthew.

"Today we are going to work on the flutter kick. Matthew, I want you to turn and face the wall. Now hold on…" I heard the sound of Matthew kicking as I ran to the bathroom fast as I could. I thought I could make it to the toilet, but just as I got there, every bit of the breakfast Momma made me eat before we left the house landed on the front of my brand-new swim trunks.

TWENTY-TWO

"Sick? What do you mean sick?" Momma asked when she picked up me and Matthew from the pool.

"I got dizzy"—I lowered my voice—"and then I threw up."

"Oh, Clem," she said. "You missed the whole lesson?"

"Momma, I was sick."

"I know, baby. It's just..." She didn't finish. I know she was thinking about how much she was going to owe Mrs. Franklin and thinking about this being my only chance to get a swim lesson.

She rubbed Matthew's head. "How was your lesson, Matthew?" she asked him real sweet.

"It was good, CeeCee." I looked up to see my momma's face, but she stared straight ahead. No matter how many times I heard it, I couldn't get used to Matthew calling my momma by a name that wasn't hers. Any Negro boy his age in his right mind would know to call my momma Mrs. Thurber, not by her first name, but not Matthew Franklin. I know that's how white folks do, but it sure doesn't make it right. But my momma didn't say a word and she wouldn't look at me even when she knew I was staring.

When we got back to the house, Matthew went upstairs

to his room and I pulled up a chair to the table in the corner to read my book while Momma worked. The radio was playing soft on the kitchen counter and right away I knew the song playing was my momma's favorite. When Momma didn't sing along with the Ink Spots and Ella Fitzgerald, her head swaying from side to side with her eyes closed like she always did, I knew she was upset.

I was reading one of the series books where the Five were surrounded by a marsh and there was a kidnapping, smuggling, and an underground passage all in one book. Every once in a while, I'd look up at Momma, scrubbing in the sink and wiping down the stove. She looked older here than at home, and all bent over.

I wanted to tell her to stand up straight like she told us when we let our shoulders droop down or we leaned on one leg, but I knew I couldn't do that. When she asked me if I was hungry, I had to remember I was supposed to be sick, so I told her my stomach still hurt and said no. Momma looked at me funny and came over and touched my head. Smelling her bleachy hands almost did make me feel sick thinking about the water.

"Well, you don't have a fever," she said.

"But my stomach still hurts," I told her, and tried to look as sick as I could.

I couldn't tell if Momma believed me or not, but she

kept on cleaning until Mrs. Franklin called her in the dining room. I could hear them talking. Well, I could hear Mrs. Franklin talking and saying "CeeCee this" and "CeeCee that," and my momma saying quiet, "Yes, Mrs. Franklin."

Right after my momma took the job with the Franklins and Errol's mom came over one night, they sat in the kitchen talking while I laid in bed listening. I couldn't hear everything they said, but I heard my momma say, "...Cecille Thurber, I told her. And do you know she had the nerve to say to me, 'Cecille? Why, that's a French name, isn't it? Why don't I just call you CeeCee, to make it easier for everyone?'"

All the way in my room I could hear Mrs. Watkins suck her teeth. "Easier for *her,* she meant. All that fancy schooling and the name Cecille is too hard for them to say? Mmmm, mmm, mmmm," Mrs. Watkins said.

Momma and Mrs. Watkins went on like that nearly every night they got together.

The next morning when Momma woke me up to go with her to work and the swim lesson, I got up slow and went to the bathroom and sat at the edge of the bathtub, staying in there as long as I could. Even though I was pretending sick, when I thought about the lesson and the pool and Daddy, my stomach started bubbling all over again.

I heard knocking on the door.

"Some of us would like to go to the bathroom this year," Clarisse started in.

I flushed the toilet and came on out.

"You're nasty. You didn't even wash your hands."

Before I could think of something to say back, Clarisse slammed the door in my face.

I walked slow into the kitchen.

"Momma, I still don't feel good," I said to Momma's back while she was at the sink.

She turned, not saying anything but looking in my eyes.

"It's my stomach," I said.

"Go on back to bed, Clem," she said, turning back to the sink. "If you've missed three lessons, I don't see how you can catch up, so we'll just have to cancel. I'll tell Mrs. Franklin."

"Sorry, Momma."

Momma was quiet. I waited for her to turn around, but she kept right on at the sink. I went back to bed, ashamed I let her down. Ashamed to not be like my daddy. But so happy I was done with swim lessons.

TWENTY-THREE

We always left for Washington, D.C., after the Fourth of July to get back in plenty of time for the Bud Billiken Parade in August, where just about everybody on the entire South Side of Chicago came out to celebrate.

The parade stretched so far down South Parkway, with bands and dancers and cars and singers, you'd think they were going to march straight out of Illinois into Indiana. I remember the first time I went with Momma and my sisters, we sat on Mr. and Mrs. Scott's stoop, Momma's friends from the NAACP, who lived right on the parade route. Momma sat me next to her and we cheered together watching folks go by in costumes. Momma laughed when I screamed loud and clapped my hands and she kept saying in my ear, "Isn't that something, Clem?" pointing to the ladies twirling sticks all stepping in time to the music of the bands playing behind them.

"Can you believe this is the biggest parade in the country, baby? Right here in Chicago?" Momma said, sounding like she was out of breath.

Momma stood me up when the shiny car with Joe Louis in the backseat drove past slow. He and his pretty wife waved to everybody and Joe Louis looked like he was in the neighborhood, just dropping by to say hello.

"He's even more handsome in person," I heard Momma say to Mrs. Scott after he passed, and Mrs. Scott nodded, yes, he sure was.

"Yeah, he may be handsome, but he got half the sense knocked out his head in the ring," Mr. Scott mumbled.

"Ooohweee, here comes that big shot Abbott in his Rolls," someone said behind us. And a long, white fancy car drove past us.

"He owns the paper," Momma said to me. I don't know which paper Momma was talking about, and I didn't care, but his car was sure pretty, and so clean it looked like it didn't have not one speck of dirt on it. Right behind were a band of young boys with caps on, playing their hearts out. Behind them, were more boys carrying sacks on their shoulders and waving their hands in the air, shouting at the crowd.

"Who are they?" I asked Momma.

"Oh, those are the *Chicago Defender* newsboys and their band, Clem. That's who the parade is for," she said, clapping and cheering them on.

I'd seen the newsboys on the corner selling papers and shouting out the words from the newspaper headlines when me and Momma walked Clarisse and Annette to school. There was one on nearly every corner we passed.

When the parade was over, everybody got free ice cream and Momma let me have two cones. I was so sticky and dirty when we got back home, I had to take an extra-long bath. I fell asleep thinking I could hardly wait for next year's parade.

Momma told us her and Daddy never missed a parade since they moved to Chicago. And once he even walked in it, holding the banner for the Pullman porters. "That night, he had to soak his feet in salts, he walked so far," she told us, "but he was proud as could be."

Since Momma started taking us, we haven't missed a parade either.

When we got on the train at Union Station my momma stood on the platform looking like she was never gonna see us again.

"We'll be back in three weeks, Momma," I told her, hugging her tight.

"Three weeks," Momma said into the top of my head. "Clarisse, watch out for them."

"I will, Momma."

She didn't have to tell Clarisse nothing. I felt bad for anyone who tried to mess with us while Clarisse was in charge. Clarisse took the tickets from Momma's hand and told her, "We'll get word as soon as we get there."

This was the first summer we were going on the train with just the three of us. Being on the train with just my sisters made me feel almost as grown as a man.

Aunt Bethel and Aunt Dorcas sent our tickets when school ended. They wrote Momma that they wouldn't be coming to get us this summer because they thought Clarisse and Annette were "mature enough to navigate the trip from Chicago," while our momma was working. I think momma thought differently but she let them send the tickets anyhow. When it comes to her sisters, they do the telling and Momma does the listening. Kind of like Clarisse with me and Annette. The tickets came with a long letter from my aunts about the plans they had for us this summer. Momma read it over dinner and I knew, like always, we were going to have our usual "aunt fun" and not the fun I'd had last summer when we went to visit Kendrick and his family in Milwaukee.

Looking at the tickets in the envelope, Momma put her head in her hand.

"Don't worry, Momma, I've been on the train plenty of times before."

Annette laughed out loud. "Clarisse. Plenty of times? We've been on the train the exact same number of times, and it ain't plenty of times."

"That's not true, Annette. Daddy would sometimes take me with him on some of his runs. I don't remember you being on the train with me then."

"I don't care how many times you've been on a train, the three of you are going to all look out for each other. You understand?"

"Is Clem going to look out for me?" Clarisse smiled at me with that sickening, sweet smile she gives when she's being mean. I smiled right back.

"Momma, wouldn't Clarisse's face scare everybody away?"

Momma got up from the table and went to the sink.

"I'll get the dishes, Momma," Annette told her. "You go sit down." Momma went into the front room.

"Can y'all just quit it?" Annette whispered to me and Clarisse. "Can't you see she's getting upset?" So me and Clarisse quit it and brought our plates to the sink for Annette to wash.

TWENTY-FOUR

The summer we went to Milwaukee was the shortest train ride I ever took, but it seemed like the longest. Momma always let me sit next to the window, and as we pulled out of Chicago, I was just about glued to the glass watching every building pass by till there were none left to see.

"Clem, why don't you close your eyes for a bit, baby? You don't want to be too tired when we get there," Momma said.

But I loved to watch the buildings as we sped past out of Chicago. Usually Momma watched with me, pointing out the buildings we knew, but this year she stayed quiet, staring straight ahead. When the porters came by and tipped their hats to Momma, I watched her eyes fill up. I slipped my hand in hers and with her other hand she reached for her handkerchief. I knew she was remembering how my daddy once worked the train, loading up passengers' bags alongside his older cousin Elwood. Momma said he rode sometimes for days at a time, traveling his route from South Carolina to Washington, D.C., stopping at every city in between. But then my daddy's cousin met his wife, and they settled down in Virginia, right outside of Washington, D.C. When my father visited them in between one of his runs, he stopped into a little coffee shop over on Eleventh Street and Florida Avenue where Momma used to eat with her friends from school. He saw Momma, "and the rest, as they say, is history." Momma always laughs at that part. Clarisse likes to fill in the other parts about them falling in love and other things I don't want to hear. Every time she tells the story she adds more like she's reading from one of her *Young Romance* magazines.

I don't know if any of what Clarisse says is true, but I know that ever since Momma met my daddy in that coffee shop she fell in love so hard, she married him just as soon as she graduated with her secretary degree from the National Training School for Women and Girls in D.C. And then they left Washington, D.C., when he got assigned to a new train out of Chicago and never looked back.

She didn't know he'd leave again when the war started. That he'd think fighting for his country was about the bravest thing a man could do for his family even if it meant leaving his wife and three children behind. I always wondered but was too afraid to ask if when he left for the navy, did Momma feel he left her behind and never looked back. After Momma finished wiping her eyes, she went off to that place she sometimes goes when she's sad.

Momma kissed each of us one last time on the platform and we hurried on. The three of us found seats in a half-empty car where we could sit facing each other. Clarisse slid in so she could sit closest to the window. Annette took the other window, and I sat down next to Annette. A good-looking young porter who barely looked older than Clarisse put our bags up on top.

"Anything else you need help with, just ask for Charles," he said, smiling right at Clarisse.

"We sure will, Charles," she said, like all of a sudden she was one of those Southern belles who fluttered their eyelashes and spoke with an accent.

I couldn't see Momma on the platform from where we were sitting, hard as I tried, but it was fine with me. I wanted to feel like we were alone and doing something grown without Momma fussing over me. I pulled out my satchel and dug around inside where I kept all my books and papers and pencils Momma got for me on Christmas and my birthday too. I took out a piece of folded-up paper and a pencil and laid it flat on my lap. For weeks, I'd been drawing a map of Washington, D.C. I started out with 67 Gallatin Street NW, where Momma grew up with Aunt Dorcas, Aunt Bethel, and her momma and daddy, who passed before I was even born. Next I put in where Momma went to school, but she said they tore that building down and put up an office building, and where she went to church every Sunday at Metropolitan Baptist Church. Next I put the White House, where President Roosevelt lives, and I drew in wavy lines for the Potomac River. Momma told me Washington has streets with numbers just like Chicago, but it has letters too, and you have to know if the street is Northwest or East, Southwest or East too. Every night when Momma got home, she helped me add just a little bit more to my map, and she told me I could fill out the rest when I got to D.C. and walked around some. Six hundred ninety-two miles from my house to Momma's house in Washington, D.C.

But what I didn't know was that by the time I left that summer, working on my map would be the last thing on my mind.

First stop out of Union Station was South Bend, Indiana, but we had barely left Chicago before Clarisse had already set up the rules.

"Clem, wouldn't you be more comfortable sitting over there?" she said, pointing to the empty seat across the aisle. Annette looked at her sideways but didn't say anything.

Clarisse looked at us both. "That way he can stretch out and work on his drawings," she said.

That's the thing about Clarisse. You never know what she's got up her sleeve. Sometimes she's being bossy like a momma for your own good and sometimes, most times really, she's being bossy for her own good. The trick is to know which is which. I took a guess that since we just left

Momma and since Clarisse just made the promise that she would look out for us, she was bossing for my own good, and I got all my pencils together and moved to the seat across the aisle. Once I got settled, Clarisse said, nice as they come, "Isn't that better?"

I didn't have time to think about Clarisse and went on back to my drawing. Annette took out a book and was reading, but I peeked out the corner of my eye and saw Clarisse looking around in her purse. First, she took out one of those little compacts that grown ladies have, and I saw her patting some powder on her face. Then I saw her put on a red lipstick and fluff her hair up.

"I'm going to the restroom. I'll be right back," she said, getting up and smoothing down her skirt. Why she needed to do all that fluffing and puffing just to use the bathroom, I didn't know, and honestly didn't much care now that I had started in good on my map.

Annette raised her eyebrows at her, then at me, and went on back to reading her book. I was glad to have the space to myself. I spread out my papers on the seat across from me, the pencils in the seat next to me. At least on this side I had my own window to look out at buildings and then fields speeding by.

"Annette!" I whispered loud across the aisle after we pulled out of the second train station. "Annette." But

Annette had already fallen asleep with the book across her chest. I had to go to the bathroom something bad. I put my pencils back in my satchel and got up, going the same way I saw Clarisse go. I walked through one car, then the next, and then I came to the dining car.

"Excuse me," I asked one of the porters, "where is the bathroom?"

He smiled, "Right through the dining car, young man," he said, tipping his hat to me. I started walking through the dining car, when up ahead I saw the young porter Charles, standing and laughing with a passenger seated at one of the tables. Her head was thrown back laughing as if he was the funniest comedian she'd ever heard. And then something about her laugh sounded familiar...

Clarisse?

I stopped in front of Charles, and he looked down at me.

"Can I help you, sir?" he asked, still smiling.

Clarisse turned around. When she saw me, she stood up quick.

"I better get going," she said.

"Now, you don't have to leave so soon?" he said, reaching for her hand.

But Clarisse tucked her hair behind her ear and smoothed down her skirt, pretending she had no idea who I was. "No, I have to go and check on my sister. Nice chatting with you," she said, her Southern belle voice back again, but she was red in the face now. She pushed past me like I was a stranger. I watched her back as she walked out of the dining car. Charles watched her walk away like he had been hypnotized.

After I used the restroom, I made my way back to my seat. Clarisse was sitting there now, her hands folded on her lap, pretending to be sound asleep.

TWENTY-FIVE

I always thought it was funny that our trip went from Union Station in Chicago to Union Station in Washington, D.C.

I remember asking Momma, "Did they run out of names for train stations?"

I made marks on my map every time I heard the conductor shout a station stop in a new state, thinking now about all the states I could mark off on my map at home, even though I hadn't really visited them, just sped through on a train. I was expecting that when we crossed into each state, I'd know it by how different they looked from each other, but Indiana, Ohio, Pennsylvania, Maryland, and West Virginia all looked about the same from the train window. But when we got to the Washington, D.C., Union Station, it looked like a busier, prettier Union Station than the Union Station in Chicago. My aunts were there waiting on the platform as soon as we stepped off, and just about snatched us away like they thought someone was going to kidnap us.

"Stay close and keep your eyes straight ahead," Aunt Dorcas told us. She grabbed my hand and Aunt Bethel grabbed Annette's. Clarisse pulled back just in time so no one could grab hold of her. I looked at Annette out the corner of my eye. She looked about as scared as I did. We marched like that all the way to my aunts' car parked out in back of the train station.

When we pulled up in front of their brick building, I thought how lucky Momma was to have grown up here in a house all her own with no landlord coming to collect the rent each month. She told me her daddy bought this house when she was younger than me, working seven days a week as a chauffeur for a white family and saving every penny.

"Working to buy that house just about killed my daddy," Momma told us one night sitting on couch when we looked at old photographs of her and her sisters and Momma and Daddy standing in front of the building. The picture was fuzzy, but my granddaddy stood tall and proud in the back row, his arm around my grandmomma. "But he wanted us to have something of our own." After her momma died, my momma lived here with Aunt Dorcas and Aunt Bethel, just the three of them in this big ole house. Momma told me her sisters take in boarders from time to time, and they both tutor students, saving every penny, just like their daddy. That with their teaching jobs, they make out okay.

"Why didn't they ever get married?" Clarisse wanted to know.

"Never had the time, I guess." Momma breathed out

heavy. "They spent all their time working and running from here to there. You know Dorcas, she always has to be in charge of everything." Momma laughed. "Chapter president of the National Council of Negro Women, chapter secretary of Delta Sigma Theta…"

"Never had the time or no one ever asked them?" Clarisse asked.

Momma looked at her. "Well, they had suitors now and again. I guess none they ever wanted to marry."

"That's sad," Clarisse said, shaking her head.

"Is it?" Annette asked her. "Sounds to me like they have a good life."

"A good life with no husband?" Clarisse said.

I looked at Momma, wondering if Clarisse was making her feel bad with all the "no husband" talk, but Momma kept right on.

"Girls," Momma said. "You never know what God has in store for you. You just have to have faith and make the best of whatever you are given." Momma got up to clear the table.

"I'm not sure I'm going to get married," I said, trying to make Momma feel better.

Clarisse laughed. "Everyone knows that Clement—Clem…" Clarisse looked up at Momma to make sure she hadn't heard her about to call me by that nickname. "No one is going to marry you," she whispered.

"I heard you, Clarisse," Momma said from the sink. "You need to focus more on your schoolwork and less on talking about marriage."

"I am, Momma," Clarisse said in her fake voice. When Momma turned on the water at the sink, Clarisse mumbled under her breath, "But I am sure not going to be some old spinster..." and Annette sucked her teeth.

The front room of my aunts' house, which they call the parlor, almost looks like the George Cleveland Hall Branch library back in Chicago with shelves stacked tall with books on top of books.

Except their books don't look like the ones I like to read, and they're mostly covered in dust and packed in tight. I once asked Miss Cook at the library if she'd read every single book on the shelves and she laughed out loud.

"I wish I had the time to read every one, Clem. By the time I finish one stack, there's a whole new stack to read. I just can't keep up."

When I thought about spending all day working at the library like Miss Cook, I thought that must be about the best job in the world. After that day at the library, I got home and told Momma I wanted to be a librarian when I grow up. She looked at me funny and told me that being a librarian wasn't a job for boys. And, besides, "a librarian's job is not sitting at a desk reading books all day. They do a lot of other things too." I didn't ask what other things they do since Momma told me boys can't be a librarian.

I knew my aunts weren't librarians. They're high school teachers. Aunt Bethel teaches English and Aunt Dorcas teaches history, but the last thing I was going to do was ask and get either one of them started on the subject of teaching or I'd be sitting up all night listening to them preach about "the value of education." The one thing I know about teachers is that they must do a lot of learning in college because when they graduate, they think they know every dang thing. They are about the knowingest people on earth in the classroom and outside it too. Twenty-four hours a day they're teaching. Every time we walked out the door with our aunts, it was a geography lesson. When we ate at a restaurant, it was a math problem. And Lord we could barely pass a street without a history lesson and one of them pointing out where Mary McLeod Bethune or Paul Laurence Dunbar lived. And just look over there because that is where Langston Hughes worked as a busboy.

"He lives in Chicago," I added, trying to show I "valued education" and knew something about history and Langston Hughes too because he sometimes spoke at the George Cleveland Hall Branch library. But Aunt Dorcas didn't want to hear none of what I wanted to add.

She stopped and looked down at me with her big hands on her hips. "But he lived in Washington, D.C., *first*," she told me. "And this is where his writing was *first* discovered."

I shut up then. I could hear Clarisse laughing behind me. One thing I learned about teachers, they don't want to hear nothing you have to say.

"You think they're gonna let us do anything fun?" I asked Annette one night after dinner when they had us washing up the dinner dishes while they sat in the front room talking to Clarisse. Seemed our aunts had a lot of ideas about what Clarisse should be doing about "her future." More ideas than Clarisse.

"They think this *is* fun," Annette said, smiling.

"If this is fun, I hate to see what their bad time is like," I said. Me and Annette laughed loud. Aunt Dorcas yelled from the front room.

"Now are you all laughing or washing dishes, because you can't do both!"

"We can't?" I whispered to Annette.

She put her soapy finger to her lips, telling me to be quiet.

"They told Clarisse tomorrow they got a special surprise planned for you," she whispered.

"I feel a stomachache coming on," I whispered, holding my belly. Me and Annette held our laughs behind our hands.

The next morning after breakfast, Aunt Dorcas told

Clarisse and Annette that Aunt Bethel was taking them shopping for a few things for school and Aunt Dorcas was going to take me someplace else.

"Can't I go shopping too?" I asked. I was scared to be alone with Aunt Dorcas.

"Now, I know my sister taught you better manners than that!" Aunt Dorcas shouted at me.

"I think Clem is just wondering where he's going," Clarisse said. About once a year Clarisse ain't so bad.

"That's why they call it a surprise," Aunt Dorcas said, a little bit nicer. "You'll find out when we get there."

TWENTY-SIX

My surprise had nothing to do with history or geography, math or reading. And it definitely didn't have nothing to do with shopping.

Aunt Dorcas leaned down. "Your mother tells me you are interested in joining the navy like your father. Well," she said, pointing down the end of Georgia Avenue, "we are going to get you navy ready."

As we walked closer, I could hear the sounds of kids screaming and laughing. And I heard the sound of water splashing.

"This is Banneker Pool," my aunt told me. "I signed you up for swim lessons."

I stopped dead in the middle of the sidewalk. "Swim lessons?" I asked.

"Your mother told me that you were sidelined by your first swim lessons, so I signed you up for some here."

I knew there was probably a history lesson in here somewhere, and I didn't have to wait long before she started. "The Banneker pool first opened in…"

But I wasn't listening to anything she said. Because I

knew that if we were going to a pool, it meant water and it meant swimming.

"But...I..."

"I think what you mean to say is 'Thank you, Aunt Dorcas,'" she said, staring down at me.

"Thank you, Aunt Dorcas, but I don't...I'm not..."

"How do you expect to join the navy if you don't swim?" She tried her best at a smile.

I didn't have an answer for that. So I tried something else. "I don't have any swim trunks."

"Clemson, I've got them right here," she said, patting a bag I just now noticed, "along with a towel."

We were at the entrance now and I could see kids big and small all lined up waiting for lessons to start.

"Hurry up and get changed. I'll be waiting over there." She pointed to the seats around the pool. I could see there wasn't no way of getting around Aunt Dorcas.

I turned and walked into the locker room, praying for anything to make me not get sick and not be afraid. Anything to make me as strong as Daddy.

I moved as slow as I could, changed into the swim trunks Aunt Dorcas brought me, and then put my towel around my shoulders to stop the shivering that had nothing to do with the cold. Aunt Dorcas was sitting dead center. Waiting. I made my way to the pool.

At Banneker Pool, everyone was Negro, even the teacher and his assistants. The teacher was old, but his assistants all looked like they were about the same age as Clarisse. And instead of just me and Matthew Franklin, there was a whole line of kids waiting for the lesson to start. I was hoping Aunt Dorcas would turn and look away so I could sneak into the bathroom, but every time I looked back at the seats, she was looking right back at me.

I made my way to the end of the line and stepped down the ladder and into the pool. I looked up at the sun and over at the buildings across the street, anyplace except at the water in front of me. The assistants spread out across the pool and when the swim teacher told us to turn to the wall, I closed my eyes tight, grabbed the ledge, held my breath, and started kicking.

"Son?" I heard behind me. I kept kicking. "Son?" I stood up, turned around, and opened my eyes. The teacher was standing behind me with his hands on his hips. "You've got to let me give the instructions before you start doing your own thing. We're gonna start with floating, not kicking. So all that splashing around you're doing isn't going to help you much when I need you to be on your back like everyone else." On either side of me, kids were standing covering their mouths trying hard not to laugh out loud. "Now I want you to face the wall, take a deep breath, arms by your side, and lean back into the water."

I stood still.

"Did you hear me, son?"

"Yessir," I told him.

"Go on now. Come on back. Real slow," he said again. On either side of me the other kids were on their backs, some struggling to stay up, but they were all at least trying to float.

I couldn't move.

I saw a big shadow above me. Aunt Dorcas.

"Is there a problem here, Clemson?" I didn't say anything. She looked at the instructor. "Give us a minute." To me she said, "Get on up out of that pool."

Aunt Dorcas didn't care who heard when she started in on me about "acting like a fool," and how she signed me up for "swim classes, not vaudeville hour." I didn't even know what vaudeville hour was, but I didn't think it was a good idea to tell Aunt Dorcas that, so I just nodded my head up and down like I knew she wanted me to, until it looked like she ran out of things to say. I didn't know where Clarisse and Annette were shopping with Aunt Bethel, but I was betting wherever they were, they could hear every word Aunt Dorcas was shouting. I didn't know what was worse, getting in the water or listening to her scream. I picked the water.

"Should I get back in the pool now?" I asked her.

"Are you ready to swim and not waste my time and

money?" I always wonder why grown folks ask questions they don't want answers to, but I shut up about that too.

I got back into the pool, but all I really wanted to do was to get back on the train to Chicago and see my momma and tell her maybe I wasn't so sure about joining the navy, especially if swimming made me think of my daddy getting blown into a million and one little pieces floating on the bottom of the Pacific Ocean.

When the teacher told me this time to lean back, I closed my eyes tight again until I felt the back of my head touch the water. My stomach bubbled and I started grinding my teeth together. He put his hands on my shoulders and tried to pull me down, but I stood up quick. I saw Aunt Dorcas walking over and he turned me toward him and said soft, "Listen, son. A lot of people are scared of being in the water. You just happen to be one of them. I'm not going to let you drown. But if you don't at least look like you're trying, that woman over there is going to drown you herself, so work with me a little bit, okay?"

I nodded with my teeth chattering.

His voice was low and deep. "Now I want you to hold on tight to my hands." I reached out under the water and grabbed his hands. He smiled at me.

"That's it, son," he said. He squeezed my hands back. "Now all I want you to do is to lean forward and put your face in the water. Like you're back at home washing your face in the washbasin in the morning."

"M-my washbasin ain't this b-big," I stuttered.

"Well, let's pretend it is. Close your eyes if you want. Don't worry, son, she can't see you."

I leaned forward until my chin was touching the water.

"Just a little bit more. This way you'll start to get used to the water."

My mouth was half-open, and I swallowed some of the bleachy water and coughed. Then I leaned forward some more. Just a little bit more and my whole face was in. I stood up, dizzy.

"There you go! You did it," the teacher said, clapping me on my shoulder. "Let's try that again."

He told me his name was Mr. Harrington, and he said he had a grandson just my age. He stayed with me that class and all the rest, helping me get used to the water. I don't know what the other kids were doing. Probably floating and swimming laps back and forth, getting ready for the Olympics, but I was dipping my face in and out of the water like I was washing up for school. I never had a grandfather in my life, but if I did, I'd want him to be just like Mr. Harrington, protecting me from Aunt Dorcas.

After our first lesson ended, Mr. Harrington got out of the pool and went over and had a long talk with Aunt Dorcas. I could see her nodding her head back and forth, then finally up and down, her hand on her hip the whole time. On the walk home, Aunt Dorcas didn't say nothing more to me about the swim lesson. I'll never know what he said to Aunt Dorcas, and I'm not sure I even care.

When we got back to the house and everybody asked how I liked my surprise, I smiled and told them I had a swim lesson. Aunt Dorcas walked straight into the kitchen. And neither of us said nothing more to each other about it. Every day she brought me back to the swim lessons for the whole week she paid for, and all I did was dip my face in and out of the water like a baby while the other kids learned to swim. If she was mad, she didn't say it, but she didn't sit and watch. I was grateful to Mr. Harrington for not making me feel like a baby. He said his job wasn't to teach me to swim, but to make sure I was comfortable enough in the water so that one day I could swim. I thought that was a nice way of saying couldn't no one teach me how to swim. But I was grateful to be able to put my face in the water without getting dizzy and grateful that when my face was in the water, even Mr. Harrington couldn't see me crying.

When we got back on the train to go back to Chicago, Aunt Dorcas and Aunt Bethel saw us off at the train platform. I could see on Aunt Dorcas's face when she hugged me a quick goodbye that being a pretend momma, even if it was just for a couple of weeks in the summer, was a lot more than she bargained for.

TWENTY-SEVEN

It wasn't so much that I was looking forward to starting seventh grade at Haines Junior High School, but after failing twice at swimming lessons, I couldn't wait for summer to be over and school to start.

Clarisse and Annette went to Haines Junior High School when they were my age, so I felt like I knew everything there was to know about it. Miss Robins was their teacher at Haines, and I knew she wasn't their favorite but just about every teacher I had liked that the answers on my tests were right and my homework was handed in neat and on time and I liked to raise my hand in class, so I knew Miss Robins would like me too. Just like I always did, I sat up front and when Miss Robins took attendance that first day and called out "Clemson Thurber," I was sure she'd ask, "Are you Clarisse and Annette's brother?" like most of the teachers did back at Lincoln Elementary. But when I raised my hand and told her my name, she kept right on calling out names like she never heard the name Thurber before when Annette sat right here in this classroom not three years ago.

Every morning, the first thing I did was put my homework on Miss Robins's desk to collect, but I never saw Errol add his to the pile. There wasn't much me and Errol talked about, and we sure didn't talk about our schoolwork, homework, or our subjects. That's the difference between boys and girls. Boys don't need to talk something to death to know how it works. Me and Errol had "different ways," as Momma put it. All the talking in the world wasn't going to change that.

In our classroom, Miss Robins loved asking questions. And I don't think there's anything she loved more than asking questions she thought we didn't know the answers to. But when I raised my hand, stretched as high as I could get it, Miss Robins looked right past me. I started to wonder if she needed eyeglasses, the way she never seemed to see me but called on kids whose hands were laying on their desks. When I shouted out my answers instead of raising my hand, Miss Robins, knowing full well they were right, shouted back, "That will be enough for now, Clem."

It wasn't that I liked Miss Robins and her mean self, always shouting and looking like she'd rather be anyplace else except standing in a colored classroom in Chicago. I pictured her getting into her car when school let out and driving as fast as she could out of the Black Belt and into her White Belt, or whatever white folks called their neighborhoods where Negroes didn't dare walk their streets, and taking a long, hot, soapy bath as soon as she got home every day. But one of the things I loved about Miss Robins's classroom was the big ole map and countries shaped like a jigsaw puzzle in all different colors.

At home I had a small map of the United States on the wall of my bedroom. Momma bought it for me just after my daddy died and I couldn't stop asking her where California was. But I still like this big map up in front of the classroom that pulled down, with all the countries in the world.

After Daddy died, Momma brought home my little map and spread it out on the table and told me a map is like a picture of the world and made a big circle around the state of Illinois and a smaller one around Chicago. And then she did the same thing for California and San Francisco.

"California is a lot bigger than Illinois," I said, looking close at all the states in between.

"Your daddy said he could get lost in San Francisco going around the corner," she said, her eyes looking soft and wet. I didn't want to start getting her worked up again, so we went back to the map. And then my momma took out a pencil and went and got Clarisse's ruler from her room and drew a long line from Chicago to San Francisco. She showed me how to look at a map and figure out the miles between the two places using the scale. I've been good at numbers since before I could read so that didn't take too long and she had me write down the numbers on a paper. "Two thousand three hundred forty-one miles," I said.

"That's it," she said, smiling.

"Is there a map for every place in the world?" I asked her.

"Sure is," she told me. "But this one here is just for this country." My momma learned how to be a secretary at the National Training School in Washington, and she didn't have nearly all the college my Aunt Dorcas and Bethel had, but she is sure a better teacher than Miss Robins.

So when I sat up in front of the class, it meant I could hear whatever it was Miss Robins was talking about, without the boys in the back of the class talking over her about last night's ball game and girls, and the girls in the back talking about their hair and boys. Up front it was Ruby, Francine Myers, Reverend Maynard's daughter Rachel, Geraldine Harris, and me. Until one day, another boy showed up, and he didn't go nowhere near the back rows like most do but took a seat two rows over but right up front near me. With his overalls and slow-talking ways, he looked like he could barely spell Chicago, let alone find it on a map. It didn't take long before the whole class started calling him Country Boy, but Miss Robins said he had just moved here from Alabama, and she said his name was Langston.

TWENTY-EIGHT

After Curtis Whittaker, Country Boy was about the biggest boy at Haines Junior High School. Some days I'd watch him when I got to my seat in the morning. And some mornings I think he got there even before Miss Robins, just waiting for class to get started, in his old farmer overalls, coming apart at the edges. I never spent much time in the South besides visiting my daddy's family that summer in South Carolina when I was barely old enough to remember, but I wondered if that poor old Country Boy could even read.

"He's got to be a farmer's son, right?" I said to Errol, walking to school one morning.

"Why don't you ask him?" Errol said, kicking at the cement.

I wasn't about to ask Country Boy if his daddy was a farmer, but I kept watching to see what else I could find out.

It didn't take me long to see that not only could Langston read, he could write too. And it looked like he wasn't so bad with numbers either. Ruby sat behind him in class, and I think she was a little sweet on him. She just about talked him to death. But he acted like he didn't hear a word, just kept his eyes on Miss Robins and the lessons.

Just like me, he handed in all of his schoolwork, with big loopy letters, his paper always folded neat in half. When Miss Robins was talking, Langston looked like he was sitting in the front row at an American Giants game, leaned forward like he didn't want to miss a word she said. Now I really did feel like a private eye, watching every move he made.

The boys in back started in on Langston early, but it was partly his own fault. His first mistake was, he didn't even try to talk to anyone. New kids come to our school all the time, and everybody knows, the first day you go out to recess, you gotta make your way over to the other boys, get a feel for things, see where you fit. But Langston didn't do none of that. Him and his slow-talking ways didn't say nothing. Just stayed to himself.

I'm not sure who started calling him Country Boy first. But it didn't take long before that became his name. Mostly everybody has a name in school. You sure don't get to pick them, but once you get them, ain't no getting rid of them.

One day when Clarisse and Annette came to the school to leave the apartment key with me before they went to their hair appointment after school, I just about dropped to my knees, praying to God Clarisse didn't start talking that "Clementine" mess in front of everybody, and then I'd be stuck with that name till I graduated from high school. But the boys were so busy smiling at the two of them, Clarisse could have called me Mickey Mouse and I don't think they would have noticed.

In our class we had a Bulldog, an Egghead, a Four Eyes, and a Pisser, just because one day, back in third grade, Martin Barclay peed his pants before he made it to the bathroom. And now we had Country Boy.

At first, Langston was like me, raising his hand every chance he got when Miss Robins asked a question she didn't really want an answer to. But every time he answered, she'd say, "I'm sorry, Langston, could you repeat that, I didn't understand you."

Of course, everybody just about fell out laughing. You know you're country when the teacher can't understand a word you're saying. Pretty soon, Country Boy stopped raising his hand, but he still leaned forward listening to every word Miss Robins said like his life depended on it.

Langston moved as slow as he talked, dragging his big self up and down the stairs like he was never in a hurry. But when the school bell rang at the end of the day, he was packed up and out the door so fast, I wondered if he had a Superman costume under those overalls.

There's not too many people I don't talk to. And if it wasn't for Lymon, there's a good chance I might have tried to talk to Country Boy too. Looked to me like we had more in common than we didn't. We were the only two boys who sat anywhere near Miss Robins. The only two handing in our homework every single morning. And definitely the only two who could answer all her questions, even when she didn't want us to. But Lymon had it in for Langston since day one. First, I thought it was his country ways. But the more I stayed quiet and watched, the more I could see, the way Lymon treated him didn't have nothing to do with Country Boy and just about everything to do with Lymon.

TWENTY-NINE

Lymon could barely eat his lunch, he was so busy looking at Country Boy.

"You see him and his daddy first day of school?" he asked us.

Errol kept eating and shook his head no.

"How'd you know it was his daddy?" I asked Lymon.

"Phhhhtt." He laughed, sounding just like Uncle Kent. Some of his sandwich flew out of his mouth. "His daddy looked about as big and country as he does." I looked over at Country Boy, sitting by himself eating. He looked so sad he made me think of the way my momma looked some mornings.

When Country Boy got up from his seat, Lymon stood up too.

"Watch this," he told us. Just as Country Boy was making his way to the trash can, Lymon pushed past him, making him fall back. Half the lunchroom started laughing. Lymon came back to our table smiling big.

"Country Boy ain't too steady on his feet," he said, and went back to eating. I looked over at Errol, waiting for him to say something, but I didn't know what. But he just looked up at Lymon, smiling. The two of them looked like they just invented a new game called Country Boy Kick the Can. I was glad I wasn't eating, because I was sure my stomach would have started bubbling by now.

"C'mon, let's go," Lymon told us, and we all stood up. It never mattered if we were finished or not, soon as Lymon said it was time to leave, it was time to leave.

Back in the classroom, Miss Robins started in on us about "How many times do I need to tell you to settle down when coming back into the classroom?" And "Are you in junior high school or kindergarten?" But that only made the class more riled up. It didn't take much to get Miss Robins yelling and her face to go red, so I think most of us didn't even listen anymore. But because today was Friday, that meant it was spelling test day and just about everyone was looking for a way to put off taking it. Except me, the girls up front, and now Country Boy. His paper and pencil were lined up neat on his desk and he was sitting still in his desk looking straight ahead at Miss Robins, waiting. I turned in my seat, hoping no one else noticed, because it was going to be worse for him on the school yard if anybody did. But everyone was still horsing around and that got Miss Robins shouting again. Finally, she started reading aloud the spelling words, and the class was silent, writing down answers. I looked over at Country Boy, writing down every word as soon as Miss Robins called it out.

"Eyes on your own paper, Mr. Thurber," Miss Robins said like I was trying to cheat. It made me so mad I nearly yelled back at her, but I kept my eyes on my paper after that. When we handed in our tests, I saw his big sloppy writing had filled in every line where a lot of kids left them blank. Country Boy is like the opposite of one of my mother's mystery books. He ain't so easy to figure out just by looking at him.

"What are we waiting for?" I asked Lymon, the first day he asked us to stay with him in the school yard after school.

"Just waiting on someone," he told us.

Errol shrugged his shoulders. He'd found a ball over in the bushes in the corner of the school yard near the fence and was bouncing it off the wall. I sat on the steps. Finally, the door opened and out walked Country Boy.

"Took you so long?" Lymon yelled when he saw him, just like Curtis used to say to me and Errol. I wondered if there was a school for bullies, so they all knew just what to say.

Country Boy acted like he hadn't heard, pulled his satchel close, but I could see his mouth get tight around the corners and his shoulders hunch up. He started walking fast. Lymon hit my arm and waved me on. I turned to Errol. "Come on," I said, walking behind Lymon.

Lymon walked up close behind Country Boy, trying to

make fun of his accent. Me and Errol laughed along like he wanted us to. And then Lymon reached out and slapped the back of Country Boy's neck. Country Boy was so much bigger than Lymon, I waited for him to turn and bust him in his lip, but he just kept right on walking. But then Lymon stood in front, and we stood behind. Lymon shoved Country Boy into us, and we shoved him back. He was like a big ole rag doll, with us shoving him back and forth like he didn't mind at all. The more we shoved and the more he took it, the madder I got. Finally, Lymon hit him good one more time and let him go.

Walking home, Errol and Lymon laughed about Country Boy's face when he saw Lymon waiting for him in the school yard. "Wait till he sees what I got for him tomorrow," Lymon said to Errol.

For the first time since we became the Three Musketeers, I was quiet. Looking at Country Boy in his run-over shoes, sitting at lunch all by himself, looking like he was someplace as far away as my momma on her window-watching mornings, didn't make me feel like laughing. When Errol and Lymon looked over at me and asked what was wrong, I mumbled something about being sick of Negroes and their country ways, and then I started right in laughing with them, like nothing at all was wrong with pushing and hitting on a boy who wouldn't even fight back.

THIRTY

The very last person I expected to see standing behind me at the library was Country Boy. I looked up from Miss Cook stamping my books and the two of us stared at each other like we'd both seen a ghost.

"You boys know each other from school?" Miss Cook asked us, and wouldn't neither of us say we did.

Here in the library, Country Boy didn't look like the same boy who sat near me in class. He was big in school, but here, he looked like a giant. At school he looked like he didn't fit, but here standing in the library room, he looked like he was right where he belonged. He had books in his hand, he was smiling, and he looked like there wasn't no place he'd rather be than standing here in front of Miss Cook's desk. I looked at Miss Cook looking at Country Boy, and it seemed she knew him about as good as she knew me. When I left, he followed out behind me up the stairs. I felt like I did with Curtis all over again, and I walked as fast as I could, but he still caught up with me at the top of the stairs. When he snatched my arm, yelling at me to stop following him, I just about laughed in his face.

Country Boy was so dumb he didn't even know what the word *following* meant.

"Ain't you the one chasing behind me?" I said, scared but smiling like I wasn't.

Scared as I was, I had to know. "This where you come after school?" I asked, feeling bad about all the times I sat waiting for him in the school yard with Lymon and he never showed up.

Langston nodded, probably not sure how to answer.

Here in the stairway, I was hoping Country Boy didn't see me the same way he saw Lymon and Errol. He took a minute, but then he answered. I kept on talking, going on about everything I knew about the library till I saw he was looking a lot less mad.

"I gotta get on home," I told him. And he didn't say nothing else. All the way back I thought about Country Boy, standing up to me like he never did to Lymon. How by myself, I guess no one in their right mind would be afraid of me. And I wondered why he never stood up for himself in the school yard. Why did he let Lymon go on beating up on him every day and not fight back? Big as he was, he had to know he could have knocked Lymon clear into tomorrow if he wanted to, but he just stood there and took it.

Country Boy might have been at the library, but he was just as dumb as I thought. I didn't know what they taught in those country schools, but they sure weren't teaching common sense.

When I climbed the stairs to my building, I thought again about him running up behind me, mad and grabbing my arm. I stopped. Country Boy didn't fight back in the classroom or in the school yard no matter how much Lymon bothered him. But he fought back hard at the library. It seemed to me like Country Boy would fight when he had something he wanted to protect.

I thought it was that I couldn't find the words to tell Lymon I was tired of beating on the other kids or tell Errol to his face that I didn't want to walk with him to school anymore, but the truth was, I needed more than words to make my mouth say those things.

When my stomach started acting up every day, Momma had me stay home from school to rest. But I felt worse when she had to call out of work to stay home with me.

"Momma, I'm old enough to stay home by myself," I told her.

"Now, what if something happens to you while I'm at work?" she asked, looking worried. "Seems like every day you are having some kind of stomach problem. I wonder if I should take you to see the doctor."

"I don't need a doctor. And it doesn't happen every day. I'll be fine, Momma," I told her.

But the next day, when my stomach still wasn't right and she couldn't call out a second day, she had Mrs. Marshall check in on me from time to time and make sure I was alive until Clarisse and Annette got home.

Being home by myself all day made the day stretch longer than I ever remembered, but it gave me time to think about going back to school.

Last year all I wanted was for kids to look up to me, maybe even be afraid of me like they were of Lymon. But now, at Haines, with no one but Errol and Lymon to talk to, and kids in sixth grade walking wide out of our way, not even looking me in the eye, I felt ashamed. Guess it was that I didn't want people looking down on me more than I wanted people looking up to me. Lymon and Errol didn't even seem to notice. They looked like they were having the time of their lives, knocking over this one and that one. Teasing and pushing. When I hung back, they looked like they'd start in on me too if I didn't join in.

Lymon still wasn't talking about what was going on with him at his house, but he told us about his daddy back in Milwaukee, traveling all the time with his music. And a grandpa who passed away. And I knew enough about Errol's daddy to know I didn't care for his kind. Lymon and Errol had daddies that were either not around when you needed them or around too much when you didn't want them. But good or bad, what both of them had was something I never had long enough to remember. A daddy.

And now when I needed my daddy more than ever before, I had no one I could ask how to be brave. How to be a man and fight for myself. All I had was a momma and two sisters. And two friends who thought I was something I wasn't.

The tears started before I could stop them. I turned over in bed, holding my stomach. On the bedside table was one of the pictures of my daddy my momma keeps in a frame and I stared at it hard, hoping to find another memory of him. Something that would help me to be stronger when I went back to school. But when I looked at my daddy, it was like I was looking at a stranger in a uniform. Like a picture of a handsome man in a magazine. Momma told me once my daddy said the toughest decision of his life was deciding to go into the navy and leaving behind a good-paying job and his family. But it was a "sacrifice" she told me he said he had to make. I couldn't spend the rest of junior high school in bed, so maybe that meant I had decisions of my own to make too. For a person with so much to say, when it came time to say something that really mattered, it seemed I couldn't say nothing at all.

My pillowcase was wet, so I flipped it over to the dry side. I thought about what Kendrick told me about boys not crying, and I tried to do what he said and think of something that made me mad. First, I got a picture of Curtis's face in my head, but that only got me partway there. Even without looking at his picture, again and again, I saw my daddy's face. I sure didn't feel mad at him, at least I didn't think I was. But when I thought again about Kendrick and my cousins in Milwaukee, even Errol, I could feel some mad starting up inside about how they all had a daddy and I didn't. Kendrick was right, though. The tears stopped, but now I felt something worse.

No matter how hard I cry or don't, I am never going to have my daddy back again. I don't have his good looks. I can't swim. And I sure don't have his bravery.

I don't know if I'm "good folk," the way Uncle Kent talked about my daddy. There ain't nothing brave about beating on someone who doesn't want to fight back. And I know nothing makes me feel like "good folk" when I'm being mean to people who've never done one bad thing to me.

Clemson Thurber Junior. I was hoping Daddy left more of him behind than just his name. Enough that I could feel more like Clemson than Clementine. Than Clem. More than just half his name and just half of my daddy.

THIRTY-ONE

Weeks after the teasing and pushing and shoving, one day after school, when Country Boy yelled in Lymon's face, "Leave me alone," Lymon got himself so worked up, he went and busted Country Boy's lip wide open. I was proud that finally Country Boy stood up for himself, but after seeing what Lymon did to him, I didn't think he ever would again. When Lymon got sent to the principal and missed two weeks of school, me and Errol went back to just being me and Errol. We walked to school quiet. At lunch I talked while he nodded. Something was missing without Lymon in the middle. Lymon was what made me and Errol stick, and without him, it was like we came apart again.

"Didn't know you could be suspended for so long," Errol finally said one day.

"Me neither. Maybe he ain't coming back."

Errol looked like I slapped him.

"Why you say that?" he asked loud.

"I don't know. Just seems strange. You ever know anybody to get suspended for two weeks for hitting someone in a school yard? Curtis almost killed someone, and he got three days," I said.

Errol nodded.

"Maybe we could stop by his house."

Errol sounded so sad, I almost felt bad for him. Almost.

"He sent you a birthday card with his address on it?" I asked Errol. "Because I sure don't know where he lives, do you?"

Errol shook his head no.

Lymon never let us see much of him past school. We walked together as far as Prairie, and then he walked off alone to his apartment.

I didn't have the heart to tell Errol the truth. That for the first time in a while, school had started to feel like school again. Without Lymon, we didn't pay Country Boy or anyone else any mind. My stomach stopped hurting, and in the hallways, kids nodded hello again. As annoying as Miss Robins was, I'd forgotten how much I liked being in the classroom, especially during social studies when she pulled down the map and I could think again about all the places I'd visit once I joined the navy.

But the best part was that when I went to the library, I saw Country Boy. Only he wasn't Country Boy anymore to me because he told me to call him Langston. So I did and even though his country accent was so strong that sometimes I had to take a minute to figure out what he was saying, once

I did, I was surprised at what I heard. I hadn't figured out yet how many miles Alabama was from Chicago, but me and Langston got along like we'd been neighbors all our lives.

But two weeks ain't no kind of time when you think about it, because just as soon as I was getting used to things going back to normal, I walked into class, handed in my homework on Miss Robins's desk, and heard behind me,

"Miss me?"

And there was Lymon.

"I thought someone kidnapped you and took you back to Milwaukee." I laughed, hitting his arm.

He smiled back. He looked older, tired too. Like he had another one of those Sugar Ray Robinson mornings. "Errol cried every day you weren't here," I told him.

He laughed then.

"You didn't?"

"Nah, I was too busy ce-le-bra-ting," I said, dancing like I was at a house party.

"You a fool, Clem." Lymon laughed. He said low, "I tell you who is going to be crying. Country Boy." He nodded toward Langston's empty seat.

My stomach started up.

"Sit down, class!" Miss Robins yelled, and Lymon made his way back to his seat.

Langston rushed in and sat down just before the bell rang. I watched his face as he saw Lymon staring at him.

At lunch, sitting next to Lymon, Errol was so happy he looked like he just hit the numbers.

"But why'd you get two weeks?" Errol asked Lymon after he told us the story about getting suspended.

"I didn't get no two weeks," Lymon said. "I just took a little *extra* vacation."

Lymon nodded his head over in Langston's direction. "You know what I had to listen to from Robert all week? Because of that crybaby Negro and his daddy sitting up in the principal's office?"

That was the first time I heard Lymon mention his momma's husband by his name. The way he said *Robert* sounded like poison and I'm betting he was.

"His daddy came to the school?" Errol asked him.

As much I liked when Errol was talking, all I could think was, *Please, Errol, don't ask him anything else about Langston and his daddy.*

"Sure did. Had his daddy come up to school and talk to the principal. About me. Well, I'mma give him something more to talk about."

Ever since he came back, Lymon didn't let Langston out of his sight. When we went outside for recess, I watched

Lymon watch Langston, even while Errol was talking a mile a minute, filling Lymon in on everything he missed while he was away. I still couldn't get used to Errol saying more than two sentences at a time, and Lymon looked like he didn't hear a word he said. When I saw Langston one day walking toward Michigan Avenue, instead of the way he usually walked toward Wabash, I knew he was going to the library. Problem was, Lymon noticed too and asked if we should find out where he was going. Lymon looked at me sideways when I told him maybe we ought to leave Country Boy alone. Back when we were the Three Musketeers, and not some gang trying to scare everybody in the school yard, we could laugh and talk all the way home. Now Lymon was looking every day for someone to put a hurting on, especially Langston, and Errol was looking to help him.

"C'mon," he said, to us one day, walking over to a corner of the school yard where I saw Langston sitting, reading a book.

"Man, you must love suspension. You looking for another two weeks?" I asked, trying my hardest to laugh.

"He's gotta pay," Lymon said, and started walking toward Langston with Errol right behind.

"You gonna be the only one paying," I said.

Lymon stopped and looked at me. "What're you saying?

You want to stand over here and let someone treat you like you nothing and you just take it?"

I stared at him. Wondering if he remembered it was him who beat up on Langston every day. And it was Langston who took it. I knew right then it wasn't Langston he was mad at and fighting. It was everybody who beat on him and treated him like nothing.

"I didn't think so," he said, and kept walking. Me and Errol followed behind. I prayed Langston would look up from his book. Prayed Langston would see us coming and go inside. Prayed that just for once, Langston would do something.

But Langston finally looked up only when Lymon was standing right over him.

"What you doing over here all by yourself, Country Boy?" Lymon asked him. I could hear Errol chuckling. "Bet you and your daddy thought I'd be gone for good, huh?"

I've seen a lot of fights in the school yard. Fights with blood and cursing, and once I even saw someone lose a tooth. But I ain't never seen someone lose a fight without one punch being thrown. But when Lymon reached out, snatched Langston's book out of his hand, ripped out page after page after page, something in Langston finally came alive, like it did that day in the library. He stood up and fought back. Not for himself, but for his book. *His book.* He twisted Lymon's arm like it was a pretzel and Lymon, who never once backed down from anyone, was on one knee, his twisted-up arm in Langston's hand and tears running down his cheeks. And when I looked around, everyone was quiet. I ran for Miss Robins, who came screaming for the two of them to get inside. Errol looked like he was ready to cry too. I'd prayed Langston would do something, anything, to fight for himself. But I never expected him to do that.

THIRTY-TWO

Up above my head, the pages from Langston's book floated on the wind like leaves. No one was quiet now, everybody was laughing and acting out how Langston twisted Lymon's arm behind his back, taking turns with who played each part. But whoever acted out Lymon's part had him begging for mercy and sounding nothing like what really happened.

I reached up and grabbed some of the pages floating above me. Then I grabbed all of the ones on the cement. Pages were flying all around the school yard, and some kids grabbed a few and I snatched them back.

Lucille from our class was standing on one. "Get off me, Clem!" she yelled when I tried to move her leg. Finally, she stepped away and I grabbed that one too.

"Help me get these," I said to Errol, who was still looking at the door Miss Robins took Lymon and Langston into.

"He's gonna get suspended again," Errol said to me, not moving.

"I told him to leave Langston alone," I said, moving him out of the way to grab another page between his legs.

"*Langston?* Since when you start calling him Langston?

And why you picking up those pages?" Errol said, looking down.

I stood up with one whole handful and looked at Errol. "What did he ever do to us, to Lymon, to deserve this?"

Errol looked back at me. "He ain't got to do nothing. Sometimes that's just the way it is."

"Is it?" I asked. "Some people just deserve to be beat on, even if they don't deserve it?"

I saw Errol blink hard. Twice. Then he looked away and at the door.

"Maybe they do," he said, facing the school. Then he turned and looked at me. His eyes were dry now, and mean, daring me to say something to him. *Just think of something else. Something that makes you mad.* Errol already knew Kendrick's rules. Being mad always stops the tears. I looked back at Errol, thinking about all those nights I could hear his mother crying in our kitchen after his father hurt her. I wondered if Errol thought she deserved it too. Maybe because she stayed too long talking to my momma. Or she didn't cook the dinner the way his daddy liked. If he believed that, then I guess he did believe Langston had it coming too. I could see the teachers coming out now and knew I didn't have long before the bell rang and we'd have to go in.

"Guess we both better go on about our business, then,"

I said to him. He nodded and walked away while I raced to the corner of the school yard where I saw more pages blown up against the fence and pulled those off. Just as the school bell rang, I saw one last page up at the top of the fence about to blow away. I climbed fast as I could to grab it.

"Mr. Thurber!" I heard a teacher yell. "Get down from there this instant!"

I jumped down from the top and took one last look around to see if there were any more pages I missed. One more page, nearly ripped in two, was over in the corner where Langston was sitting. I grabbed it and ran into school before the last bell rang. Errol was nowhere in sight.

Back in the classroom, everyone was still talking about the fight like Langston was the new heavyweight champion. I heard Ruby even call Langston handsome. It was like everybody except Errol had been waiting for someone to take down Lymon, but no one was brave enough to do it.

"Settle down, class," Miss Robins said, rushing back into the room, her face shiny and bright red. But there ain't no settling down after a recess like the one we just had.

After school, for the first time, I didn't wait for Errol, I just walked on ahead by myself. It felt good to finally be alone, not trying to be funny or make up things to talk about, just think. I kept playing over in my head the fight between Lymon and Langston. Each time I did, Langston got bigger and bigger till he was almost like a giant standing tall over Lymon. When I got home, I opened the front door quiet so that Clarisse and Annette couldn't hear me and went straight to my room. From my satchel, I took out all the pages from Langston's book and laid them out on my bedspread. I flipped through them, wiping off footprints and dirt, then lining them up by page number and reading some of the words on the pages.

I couldn't count how many times I'd seen Langston by himself, in a corner at the library, or at lunch reading one of his books. Once he didn't even hear the bell ring, and Miss Robins had to go out and tell him it was time to come inside after recess. I keep my reading to myself, at home in my room, but Langston seemed like he read every place but home.

When I got all the pages in order, I put them back neat in my satchel. Lymon didn't get a chance to rip up the whole book, so I was hoping with the pages I saved, the book could still be fixed. I stretched out on my bed with my arms behind my head, tired. Just thinking about Lymon, Langston, and Errol made me want to close my eyes and wake up when seventh grade was over. But when I thought about how Langston was beat on nearly every day, the funny poems he read about *black beauty* and *thou* and *hast* and how now, after all these months, it was Langston who was a hero, my head started pounding. Just when I thought I knew the rules, something changes, making me think I don't know anything at all.

THIRTY-THREE

I waited outside in the school yard for Langston, but he never showed up. The wind was whipping up something good, but I was so proud I found all the pages to his ripped-up book, I didn't pay attention to the wind or the cold. Errol had gone on home. Neither one of us made a plan to stop walking together, but after yesterday, we both knew things between us weren't ever going to be right again. Now I just had to figure out a way to tell my momma. When the school yard was just about empty, I zipped up my jacket and started home by myself.

Today Momma told me instead of going home, I had to walk to DuSable High and wait outside while she was inside speaking to the principal, because Momma didn't want me home alone without Clarisse or Annette. I knew Clarisse was in some kind of trouble. I just didn't know what kind and how much. But it was the kind of trouble that meant Momma had to leave work early and that meant it was big trouble because if Momma lost hours with the Franklins then she lost pay. Annette was staying after school for her French Club meeting, and I don't know why anyone would want to sit around for an hour every week after school speaking in another language, but Annette said of course I wouldn't understand because it was for "enrichment." When I told her that enrichment reminded me of summers with our aunts and sounded "boring," Annette called me an *imbécile.* And I sure didn't need to speak French to know *imbécile* meant *dumb.*

I sat in front, on the steps watching high schoolers go in and out, walking down Wabash, some holding hands, all of them talking loud, and I opened my book, wondering how long Momma could take to hear bad news from the principal. I just knew it had to be something about Clarisse and her new boyfriend, Ralph. At home, I tried to listen in, but hard as I tried, I couldn't get as many details as I wanted. I did find out that Ralph went to DuSable High with Clarisse. He played on the basketball team, and of course, all Clarisse could talk about was how "fine" he was and that he was a senior, one year ahead of Clarisse. She told Annette he might have a friend for her too.

I saw him only once when Clarisse snuck him in the house before Momma got home from work. I don't know about "fine," but he looked all right. He was heads taller than Clarisse, skinny, and he barely had two words to say, but I'm not sure if that's because Clarisse doesn't let anybody say much. She was all sweetness and smiles. She was even nice to me.

"And this is my little brother, Clemson," she said, introducing us.

"Clem," I told him.

"What's up, little man?" he said, giving me skin.

His hands were big and ashy, and he had the whitest, straightest teeth, like he was in a toothpaste commercial. Clarisse gave me a look that said *get lost,* so I went in my room and waited till it was quiet, then I poked my head out and saw them in there on the couch kissing. I didn't have Annette this time to set Clarisse straight. My stomach hurt so bad thinking what would happen if Momma came home and found Clarisse in there with Ralph. I could see Momma being led off to jail after she strangled Clarisse or both of them to death. One of Momma's rules was no company when she was at work. She didn't have to say *No Boyfriends on My Couch Kissing Like You Are Grown Married Folks* for Clarisse to know that wasn't allowed either. There isn't much I hate more than lying to my momma and keeping secrets from her too, and here was Clarisse making me do both in one day. But I owed Clarisse a favor, so I shut my mouth, held my stomach, and didn't say a word.

After all the smiling and kissing with Ralph finished and Clarisse said goodbye at the door for I don't know how long, I came out to finish my schoolwork in the kitchen and pretend it was just any other day. Annette was at her French

Club meeting, so Clarisse gave me a look, daring me to open my mouth when Momma came home and asked how our day went.

"Pretty quiet, right, Clem?" she said.

"Mmmhmmm," I said.

Momma looked at us both funny, but she didn't ask anything more. I couldn't even eat my dinner.

Thinking now about Clarisse and Ralph and Momma and the principal made my stomach start up again. I got up and moved from the steps to wait inside the school.

I'd only been inside DuSable a few other times, when Momma had meetings with teachers and twice when I had to sit through watching Clarisse in a play and Annette singing in the spring chorus. I walked down the hallway where I thought the principal's office was, but I only saw classrooms and lockers, so I made a left and wound up at the gym. Just as I was turning around, I heard the sound of a whistle.

Next to the gym was a window partly fogged up. I wiped it off with my sleeve and could see some kids lined up through the blurry window. I walked around to the big double wooden doors and opened them. And then I smelled the bleachy smell that always made me sick. *A pool.*

Inside was so hot and steamy I could barely breathe. Standing along the edge with matching swim trunks were about a dozen DuSable High School boys, each one wearing glasses over their eyes with a strap around back. They stood in a line while a man with a whistle around his neck stood next to them and waved each of them into the pool. One after the other they dived in from a board at the edge, so smooth, you barely heard them hit the water. Then they would swim like fish, smooth as could be, I bet like my daddy used to swim, to the other end of the pool. They looked like a musical group, all in perfect rhythm.

"Young man!" the coach yelled to me. I looked up. "This is a closed practice for the swim team only. You'll need to leave." I stepped back, still watching.

"Come back for the meet," he told me. He whistled again as the boys began swimming back to the other end.

I turned quick and left out. Back out in the hallway the air was cool again. I found my way back to the principal's office. Momma was sitting on a chair waiting.

"Where were you?" She looked half-mad, half-worried.

"I got lost, looking—"

"Come on," she said, walking ahead and out the door. Outside, when I was waiting for Momma, I could barely wait to find out what Clarisse was in trouble for. But that was before I saw the DuSable swim team.

THIRTY-FOUR

I don't know when the house had been so quiet. When we got home, Clarisse went straight to her room, and Momma went to the kitchen to start on dinner. Annette got in from her club and came into my room.

"Ooowee, Clarisse is in trouble," Annette whispered after she closed the door.

"All Momma said on the walk home was 'Learning means using your ears and not your mouth, Clarisse,' and then she didn't want to hear nothing Clarisse had to say," I whispered back.

"Well, Clarisse ain't saying much now, but I heard she ran her mouth off to Miss Cunningham the other day."

"Who is Miss Cunningham?" I asked. I tried to keep track of all of their teachers, so I'd know who to look out for when I had them.

"She's the English teacher. Miss Cunningham may be old, but she does not play," Annette said, looking serious. In my head, I hoped Miss Cunningham was long gone by the time I got to high school.

"Anyhow, she got sent to the principal's office," Annette finished.

"So Momma had to go to the school just because Clarisse was mouthing off in class?" I asked.

"Well...," Annette said slow. "It wasn't the first time."

"So it didn't have nothing to do with Ralph?" I asked.

Annette smiled slow at me and tilted her head to the side. "What do you know about Ralph?"

"Not much," I said, wishing I had kept my big mouth shut.

"Clem-son," she said slow. "Did you tell Momma something about Ralph?"

"No! I didn't tell Momma nothing. I promised Clarisse!"

"Okay, relax," Annette said. "Just checking. Well, I guess we'll just have to wait to find out what happens next."

As she turned to leave, I said, "Annette..."

"Yeah?" She smiled. "More questions about Monsieur Raoul?" I hated when she started in on her French talk.

"No. You ever been to one of those swim meets at the high school?" I asked her.

"The swim meets? A couple of boys from my class are on the team, and my friend Linda's brother is the captain. They have one of the best records in the state. Why?"

"Just wondering."

She put her hand on her hip. "You're just wondering about DuSable High's swim team?" When Annette put her hand on her hip she reminded me of Aunt Dorcas.

"Yeah...well, no...when I was at the school today...I just didn't know they had a swim team," I stuttered.

"Well, keep up with your swim lessons and maybe I can go to your swim meets in a few years," Annette said, and of course added, "and watch you lose." She closed the door behind her, laughing.

That night in bed, I thought I'd never fall asleep, thinking about Momma and Clarisse. But just when I thought I'd be seeing the sun rise, I found myself in a big pool, swimming with my daddy.

As soon as the coach blew the whistle, the two of us dived into the pool and started swimming, racing each other to the end. At first, my daddy was out in front, swimming just like he was that day on the lake with long, smooth strokes. But the faster I moved my arms and legs, the closer I got to him. In the water, I felt as light as air, and my body seemed to know just what to do. My arms were bent at the elbows, my legs out long behind me with my feet kicking the water just like the swim team swimmers did, and my head turned to the right side for air each time my arm lifted out of the water. Standing on the edge were Momma, Clarisse, and Annette, bent down and cheering, though I couldn't tell who they wanted to win. Pretty soon I was swimming side by side with my daddy, looking right at him, our arms going in and out of the water at the same time. He wasn't wearing the swimmer's glasses, so I could see his eyes smiling right along with his mouth. *Clemson Junior,* I saw his mouth say, and he looked proud I could keep up with him. He smiled more as little by little I moved ahead, and before I knew it he was behind me, his head near my feet. When I looked ahead, the edge of the pool seemed a mile away, and when I looked behind, Daddy was too. The harder I swam, the smaller Daddy got, until finally he was so far away, I couldn't see him at all.

"Daddy!" I yelled. "Daddy!" But he was gone.

I stopped swimming. When I looked up, Momma, Clarisse, and Annette were gone too and there was just me and the coach with the whistle telling me, "Come on, son, you're almost there." But just like that I forgot how to swim. It was like my arms and legs stopped working. I could feel myself sinking to the bottom of the pool.

"Daddy!" I tried to scream. "Daddy, help!" But there was no sound because my mouth filled up with water.

I opened my eyes and took a deep breath, coughing. The light was coming through the window in my bedroom. I sat up breathing hard. The room was hot and stuffy, but I felt cold. It had been months since I dreamed of my daddy. I climbed out of bed, dizzy, and looked down. In the middle of my bed was a big wet spot. Not since I was little had I wet the bed and here I was in junior high, dreaming of my daddy, and drowning and feeling like a baby all over again.

THIRTY-FIVE

I waited again for Langston after school, but when he didn't show, I raced over to the library, thinking I could catch him before he had to go in and show Miss Cook the ripped-up poetry book. I didn't know much about Langston, but I guessed he was what my momma would call "upstanding," and would confess everything to Miss Cook like he was being tortured by the enemy in a prison camp, so I thought I'd save him the trouble. Just when I thought I'd missed him again, I saw him coming down Michigan Avenue, walking slower than ever, his hands tucked in his jacket, his head down and looking at his feet like he had to remind himself how to walk. He just about knocked me over in the doorway of the library.

"Watch where you going," I told him.

He looked up at me like he'd seen a ghost. But when I pulled all the pages torn out of his book that I collected from my satchel, I thought he was going to faint dead away.

He snatched them from my hand. "Thanks for this," he said. "I was thinking Miss Cook was gonna take back my library card."

Just when I started thinking that Langston was smart

as me, he went and said something as crazy as that. It goes to show you, there's school smart and then there's common-sense smart. Not everybody has both kinds of smarts.

"Take back your library card?" I laughed out loud but quieted down when I saw the hurt in his face.

"They don't do that. They mark the book damaged, maybe make you pay. Now that you got the pages"—I pointed to all the pages in his hands—"they can fix it."

I told him I'd come with him to tell Miss Cook what happened to his book. At Miss Cook's desk, I listened as long as I could to him, stumbling and stuttering out his words, until finally I had to help out.

"Wasn't his fault, Miss Cook, honest," I told her.

But for the first time ever, Miss Cook didn't want to hear from me. I think she wanted Langston to take *responsibility,* which is what it means when adults want you to feel more sorry about something you just said you're sorry for. And then when she finally thought Langston felt bad enough, she told him what I just told him outside, that no, she was not going to take back his library card and that because all the pages were there, the book could most likely be repaired. He couldn't stop smiling then.

I'm not sure Langston believed me when I told him I wasn't friends with Lymon anymore. And I could see

Langston still wasn't sure why I collected all those pages for him. If he came out and asked me, I just might start stuttering and stumbling the way he did with Miss Cook at her desk. I'm not sure I could have told Langston that I was done with being the kind of man that I was in the school yard. I wished Lymon and Errol could have been here with us today. That they could have seen me and Langston with each and every page of that book standing in front of Miss Cook, telling her the truth. Both of us like *upstanding* men. I'd want them to see up close that it's not always fists that win a fight.

After I gave him the pages to his Langston Hughes poetry book, I started seeing Langston just about every Thursday at the library. And I don't exactly know how it happened but first we'd be talking about one thing or the other, and I'd walk with him one block. Then it was two. Next thing I knew, one of us, I'm not sure who, started waiting for the other after school to walk over to the library. And now, here we were, every Thursday, at the library like we were long-lost friends. After the fight that wasn't really a fight in the school yard between Lymon and Langston, I couldn't pretend anymore. I saw Lymon watching us leave school and walk toward Michigan. Errol looked like he didn't care one way or the other and he probably didn't. But it was Lymon who looked like he'd lost something. But just like my daddy, I made a choice, and I was going to stick with it even if it was hard. And I made the choice to leave the Three Muske-teers behind. I decided to stop fighting and laughing when I didn't feel like laughing, and to stop teasing and pushing and being who I didn't want to be. And I chose a friend who knew what it was like to lose someone you loved, because Langston told me he lost his momma too. I chose someone who liked to read and didn't mind me talking about maps and traveling. And I chose Langston.

One Thursday, when we were walking back home from the library, I asked him something I'd never ask Lymon or Errol.

"You ever do any swimming back in Alabama?" I don't know if I was hoping he'd say yes or hoping he'd say no, but I had to know either way.

"Me, swim? Big as I am, I'd sink to the bottom like a rock I try to get out there and swim." Langston laughed. "You the one joining the navy. You must know how to swim."

I didn't say a thing and neither did he.

That was the thing about Langston. He was quiet at just the right times, not all the time like Errol.

"I'd like to learn," I said finally.

"What's stopping you?" he asked. "Seems to me, you know just about everything else."

I laughed. "Being smart in class doesn't mean I can swim."

He nodded. "Yeah, but it don't mean you can't learn neither."

Now it was my turn to be quiet. I couldn't tell Langston that learning to swim was a lot more than teaching someone how to breathe and move their arms and legs the right way.

"There's a lot more to swimming than learning to swim."

"See there, even that's too smart for me to understand." He smiled at me. "Later, Clem," he said, heading off toward Wabash.

I waited at the corner watching Langston walk off. He had to pass DuSable High School to get to his apartment, and it made me wonder if the swim team was practicing now.

I'd just about reached Prairie Avenue when I saw Errol up ahead. He was walking slow, by himself, his knapsack hanging low off his back. We still nodded at each other at school, but that's about all we did. Errol and Lymon sat on one side of the lunchroom, I sat with Langston on the other. If the four of us were on a map, me and Langston would be on one island with Errol and Lymon on another, with mountains and an ocean dividing us.

THIRTY-SIX

One thing I never wanted was my momma and Miss Watkins to stop being friends because of me and Errol, and so far, nothing much had changed. Mrs. Watkins still came up most nights, especially those times when she and Errol's daddy were fighting. I got used to the sounds of the whispering and sniffing in the kitchen and Momma telling her to leave or to stay; to fight or to stay quiet. I never knew what my momma would say to her. All I knew was whatever she told her, none of it worked, because Mrs. Watkins would be back up in our apartment the very next week, crying again.

In between the crying and the advice, they still laughed just the same. Far as I could tell, the one thing they didn't talk about was me and Errol.

I told my momma about me and Errol one Saturday at breakfast. I came in early as she was getting ready for work.

"Morning, Momma," I said.

"Oh, morning, Clem," she said, looking up from her coffee and window-watching.

"I'm gonna go to the library today," I told her.

"Okay, honey. But right there and back," she said.

"Well, I'm going with a friend," I told her.

My momma looked up. "Errol?"

"No. Langston," I told her.

"I never heard you mention a Langston."

"He's new. From Alabama," I told her, starting in on my breakfast.

"Is he a nice boy? Nice family?" she asked. I could hear the worry starting in her voice.

"Yeah, very nice. He's kind of country, though, but nice. His momma died a couple of years back, so he's here with just his daddy. But the two of us like going to the library."

"Mmmhmmm," Momma said, which meant she was thinking things over. "Does Errol like Langston too?" she asked.

I shrugged my shoulders.

"Speak up, Clem. I don't know what this means." Momma shrugged her shoulders the way I did.

"Momma...Something ain't right with Errol. We had this new friend at school and the two of them started pushing people around, especially Langston. I don't hang out with Errol anymore. Or walk to school together either."

Momma looked at me hard.

"Did Errol hurt you?" she asked.

"No...not me...but..."

"But what?" Momma said, sharp.

I didn't answer her.

"Well, let me talk to Beulah about it, and we'll get this figured out."

"Why do you have to talk to Mrs. Watkins about something between me and Errol?" I asked her.

Momma looked at me.

"Are you saying I don't have a right to find out what's going on?"

"I'm saying that just because you're my mother doesn't mean you can fix everything. Some things I can fix for myself."

Momma stood up, spilling her coffee. She looked at me like I was a stranger she just met. I know she was waiting for me to say I was sorry. To smile and get up and hug her. But I couldn't. I couldn't give in again to what Momma wanted. The coffee dripped off the table and onto the floor and Momma pretended she didn't see it and walked out of the room. I got a washrag from the sink and cleaned it up.

I don't know if she was still going to talk to Mrs. Watkins or not or if she was mad and wasn't going to speak to me. Or both. But whatever happened, I knew that I was done with Lymon, and I was definitely done with Errol.

THIRTY-SEVEN

On Saturdays, when me and Langston left the library, I walked with him to Wabash and then headed back to Prairie. Langston always had to go home first because his daddy didn't let him take off a whole day from his chores.

"You straight up got a whole day of chores?" I asked. I was ashamed to say all I had to do was clean up my room and sometimes empty out the trash and my momma and sisters did the rest.

"It ain't so bad," he said, and he sounded like he meant it. "Me and my daddy get them done pretty quick. Back in Alabama, I had to help my daddy chop firewood, feed the hogs, clean out the barn, keep up the garden. On washday, I used to draw water for my momma to—"

Langston stopped. "You know your mouth is wide open?" he said, looking at me, laughing.

"Did your momma and daddy know slavery ended in 1865?"

Langston laughed again. "Whatever thy hand findeth to do…," he started.

"…do it with thy might!" we said together.

"Ecclesiastes 9:10," Langston finished. "My daddy does not play when it comes to Scripture or chores."

"Is your daddy named Langston too?" I asked him before I could stop myself.

"My daddy? Nope. Henry." Langston laughed. "He wishes I was Henry Junior, but I am sure glad my momma chose Langston."

"I think saw your daddy once when he came to the school," I said. "Big dude, looks like your twin?"

"Yup, that's my daddy all right. We look alike, but beyond that, there ain't much else we got in common," Langston said, looking straight ahead. "Me and my momma, though…" He didn't finish.

I know my momma says I ask too many questions. And I know I should be more like Annette and do more listening, but sometimes my mouth moves faster than my brain.

"Why not?" I asked him. "Why don't you have anything in common with your daddy?"

Langston looked at me long and waited a minute before he answered. He breathed heavy. "My daddy…" Langston stopped. "My daddy thinks life is work, God, and family and that's about it. When my momma died, he lost God and almost gave up on his family."

"But you think different?" I asked him.

"I believe in those things too, but I think what makes life good is all that's in between."

"In between?" I asked him.

"Yeah," he said. "Like the library."

"And Lena Horne?" I added.

"Nah, Miss Nina Mae McKinney." Langston put his hand over his heart.

"And B-Fifty-Two bombers," I added.

"And the Brown Bomber, Joe Louis."

"And the Bud Billiken Parade," I said.

"Warm corn bread dipped in buttermilk," said Langston.

"Now, why do you have to go all Alabama on me?" I hit his arm.

We were both laughing now.

"Like I said, there's a lot in between," Langston said.

I nodded.

"Can I ask you something about your daddy?" he said, looking nervous.

"Yup."

"How old were you when…when…when the accident…" Langston looked away. I could tell he was wishing he never started asking.

"I was nine," I told him. "But even before the accident I didn't see him much because he went into the navy when I was five."

"Mmmmhmmm," Langston said, quiet as could be.

We walked another block. "I don't even remember what his voice sounded like," I said. Langston looked over at me.

"Some days, I forget what my momma looked like," Langston said. I could hear his voice change when he talked about his momma. "But I always remember her voice. The way she used to call my name. *Langston,*" he said in a woman's voice with a country accent. "I hope I never forget that."

I could feel the lump in my throat getting bigger and bigger, so I started thinking about anything other than my daddy and Langston's momma.

Langston stopped in the middle of the sidewalk. "Before my grandma passed, she told me my momma was up in heaven, and she was my guardian angel. Said she'd always be looking down on me, watching over me. Then when my grandma passed, I thought it'd be the two of them together making sure I was okay. Now…"

"Now what?" I asked him. I could hear the crying sound in my voice even though my eyes were dry.

"Maybe your daddy and my momma are looking down on the two of us. Maybe they're gonna help us get through. Together," Langston said.

Hard as I tried, I couldn't think of one mad thing to stop the tears from coming.

THIRTY-EIGHT

One week when me and Langston walked home, I noticed a big school bus standing in front of the high school that said LANE TECH.

"They making kids go to school on Saturdays too?" I laughed.

"Must be a game," Langston said. "Sometimes they're so loud, sounds like they're right outside my window."

But I knew there wasn't a basketball game today because Clarisse and Annette went to just about every one. Annette to see her friends, and Clarisse went, I knew, to see Ralph play. I was betting she sat right up front too, like she was his personal cheerleader. Momma told me I'd have to wait to go. "They're just too rowdy, Clem," she said, and that was that. I didn't ask again.

When we got out front, we slowed down.

"Let's go see," I told Langston. I wasn't ready to go back to the house and my room. I knew Langston wasn't ready to start his chores.

He smiled. "Real quick, though. My daddy'll be waiting."

Hearing him say that hurt my stomach, but I smiled through it.

We ran up the front steps of DuSable.

I walked down the hall to where I knew the lockers were and where I saw the pool. The big wooden double doors were open and all around the pool the stands were filled with people. *A swim meet.*

I nearly slipped on the black-and-white-tiled floors around the pool heading to the seats, but Langston caught my arm.

"You trying to end up in the pool, and you ain't even swimming." He laughed.

We squeezed in two seats near the front.

Swimmers from both teams were at either ends of the pool. The DuSable swimmers had on shiny blue swim trunks, so tight I'd be ashamed to be seen in them, I don't care if I was on a swim team or not. But they didn't look ashamed. They looked proud, with their broad chests, full of muscles, some with hair like grown men. The DuSable team sat on one side of the pool, the other school sat on the other. Men in white shirts holding whistles and little clocks around their necks stood on the sides. And sitting up high were the lifeguards like I see at Lake Michigan, just waiting for someone to start drowning. I made myself stop thinking about drowning and the bleachy smell and turned to Langston.

He looked like he was thinking the same thing I was about those swim trunks.

"They look like underwear," he whispered.

I nodded.

A whistle blew and boys started lining up behind stands. The whistle blew a second time and they each took a step up and stood still like they were statues. The whistle blew again, and they dived in like rockets. They stayed underwater so long I was sure they weren't coming up again, and then all of a sudden their arms rose up and lifted their bodies out of the water. There was so much splashing I could barely see who was winning, but the boy in the middle lane started pulling away. The cheers around me were getting louder and the coaches and the men in white shirts were walking fast up and down the pool alongside the swimmers, looking at their watches and at their papers. Boys on either end were screaming but I don't think there was any way the swimmers could hear them.

The boy leading was from DuSable. His arms were long and brown and came straight out of the water, made a circle, went up over his head, and went back in again. He looked like an acrobat. When he got to one end, he'd spin forward, flip over, push off with his feet, and swim underwater until he exploded out of the water again. By the time he finished in first place I was cheering just as loud as everyone else.

Langston was tapping me on my shoulder.

"Clem, I gotta go," he said through the noise.

"Now?" I asked him.

"Yup. My daddy—"

"All right," I said, getting up to go.

"You ain't got to leave," he said.

I looked to make sure he was serious. "You sure?"

"Yeah. I'd stay if I could, but…"

"All right then," I said, turning back to the meet. "See you Monday."

Langston left out, and I sat back down. The pool was still hot and stuffy, but the bleach smell disappeared. I took off my jacket and watched another set of swimmers step up. I leaned forward in my seat waiting for the whistle and the next race to start.

I got a whole education in swimming just sitting in the bleachers. First off, there were all kinds of names for swimming when I just thought you got out there and swam or you didn't. But there's a whole lot of ways to get across a pool. Breaststroke, backstroke, freestyle, and my favorite, the butterfly, the one where your arms come out of the water and make a big wide circle. It doesn't look much like a butterfly's wings, but it sure is pretty to watch. I watched so long, I was about the last to leave. I didn't know what time it was, and I knew I was going to have a lot of explaining to do to Momma when I got home, but I'd have to worry about that later.

As I stood up, the coach was by the pool, picking up towels and the glasses left behind by the swimmers.

"Hand me those goggles, would you, son?" he said to me.

I looked down at another pair of glasses near the edge of the pool.

"These?" I asked him.

He nodded.

I laughed. "You called them googles?"

He laughed back. "No, they're called *goggles*. Guess you're not a swimmer?" he said. "You have a brother swimming for DuSable?"

"Nah, just watching."

He looked for a minute. "Weren't you in here last week? I told you to come back for a meet, right?"

All of a sudden, I felt ashamed. I nodded and handed him the glasses. "See you later," I said, walking toward the doors.

"Can you give me a hand for a minute?" he asked.

"I...uh...got to get on home...," I said.

"Just be a minute," he said, grabbing at the ropes in the pool they used to make the lanes. "Everyone likes to swim, but no one likes to help clean up," he added, smiling.

"Why don't you make the swimmers help?" I asked him, unhooking one of the ropes at the end of the pool like I watched him do.

"Ahh, they're hyped up after their win. They want to get in the locker room, shower and change, go meet their friends. You know the drill."

I didn't know the drill, but I nodded like I did.

Just then one of the swimmers walked out, still in his bathing suit with a towel around his neck. I'd noticed him at the meet sitting on the bench more than he was in the pool.

"Coach. Sorry, I forgot we were supposed to help get these up," he said, grabbing the lines I was helping with.

"Too late," Coach told him. "I already got Mr.— What's your name, son?"

"Clem…Clem Thurber," I told him.

"I already got Mr. Thurber to help me." The coach winked at me.

The boy turned and looked at me. "Thurber? You got a sister at DuSable?"

"Yeah, I got a sister," I said. This was a question nearly everybody asked once they found out my last name was Thurber. "Clarisse is my sister."

"Clarisse?" he said, like he never even heard her name before. "You have a sister named Annette?"

I had to keep my mouth from dropping open. "Annette…
yes, my sister Annette," I said, sounding like I didn't even
know my own sister.

His face lit up. "Tell her Anthony says hello," he said,
flashing a smile.

"All right, Anthony, this isn't an episode of *Blind Date*,"
the coach told him. "Get over there and help Mr. Thurber
get these lane lines up." He was smiling.

"Where do you go to school, Annette's brother?"
Anthony said, flashing that smile again.

I couldn't wait to get home and see Annette's face when
I asked her about Anthony. All that talk about "I know a
couple of boys on the team" and "my friend Linda's brother."
Looked to me like Clarisse wasn't the only one with admirers.

"I'm at Haines," I told him, feeling like I might as well
have been saying I went to kindergarten.

"Haines? I went to Haines too. You planning on swimming in high school?" he asked me.

I shook my head no.

"Why's that?" he asked. We finished pulling up the
ropes, and we rolled them up neat on the pool deck.

"I don't know."

"Yeah, a lot of us go for basketball instead. Is that what
you play?"

I shook my head again.

"Thanks, boys!" Coach yelled from the end of the pool, heading into the locker room.

I thought about my decision to stop pretending to be something I wasn't.

"Because," I said, looking him in his eyes, "I'm too afraid to swim."

THIRTY-NINE

Annette had more questions than answers when I raced in the house to tell her about her Anthony.

"What were you doing at a swim meet?" she asked me.

"Why weren't *you* there if your boyfriend was swimming?" I asked her, laughing.

"Didn't you tell Momma you were at the library?"

"I went *after* I went to the library." Annette wasn't giving me anything to work with.

"Did they win?" she asked.

"You mean, did *Anthony* win?" I couldn't stop laughing.

"You really are a child, Clem," Annette said. "Anthony is in my math class, and he's in French Club with me."

"Is that where you two *French*-kiss?" Now my eyes were tearing up, I was laughing so hard.

"I don't have time for this," Annette said.

"Don't have time for what?" Clarisse said, walking into the kitchen.

"Annette's boyfriend, Anthony," I blurted out, wiping my eyes.

Clarisse looked at Annette. "Anthony? Anthony Stokes?"

"Yup," I said, though I didn't even know if that was his last name.

"I knew it!" Clarisse shouted.

"Will the two of you stop it?" Annette said, looking away.

"Wait." Clarisse turned to me. "How do you know Anthony?"

"Because he was someplace he wasn't supposed to be, sitting up at the DuSable swim meet when he was supposed to be at the library," Annette said.

"I can't go to a swim meet?" I asked them.

"Aren't you the one too afraid to even go near water?" Clarisse said. Annette hit her in her arm and they both got quiet.

"What?" I said.

Annette rolled her eyes at Clarisse. "You always have to go running your big mouth?" she said.

"So how long are we all supposed to pretend Clem ain't afraid of water?"

I stood looking at them and couldn't find one thing to say. Annette came close to me. "Momma and Aunt Dorcas said you—"

I looked at Clarisse. "I just don't like swimming!" I yelled. "Doesn't mean I'm afraid." I could feel the tears starting and I knew I couldn't cry in front of Clarisse or tell her I was afraid, or I'd be hearing about it for years.

"It's okay to be afraid of something, Clem. We all are. Right, Clarisse?" Annette said.

Clarisse looked like she wasn't sure how to answer, then nodded her head yes, but I could tell Clarisse ain't never been afraid of anything in her life.

"Yeah?" I said to them. "What are you afraid of?"

"Bugs," Annette said. She looked at Clarisse.

"Me too," Clarisse said finally.

"Is that why we always ask you to kill them?" I said.

"All right then. Sometimes I'm afraid of…" Clarisse looked around the room.

Annette laughed, "C'mon, Clarisse, everybody's afraid of—"

"Sometimes I'm afraid people won't like me," Clarisse whispered so soft we barely heard her.

"What? You?" I said. "Everybody likes you."

"Everybody *knows* me. That's different from everybody liking me," she said.

I never thought about that.

"Everybody likes Annette. Everybody likes you. I'm scared nobody likes me."

Me and Annette were quiet.

"Now you all have nothing to say?" Clarisse said to us.

"We're just surprised is all," Annette said. "Everybody likes you, Clarisse."

I nodded my head so I looked like I was agreeing with Annette, but when I thought about it, I realized Clarisse was hard to like. The way she was always bossing everybody, and half the time she seemed so mad, she looked like she'd sooner fight you than speak to you.

She shrugged her shoulders. "Well, nothing I can do if they don't," she said, heading to the icebox. "Is Momma gonna be late again?"

I took my books out of my satchel and started on my schoolwork. Annette did too. Clarisse cut up an apple, and we all sat at the table quiet. In one day I went from hiding being afraid of swimming to just about everybody knowing, and I still didn't know if there was a way to stop being afraid. It didn't look like Annette was trying to stop being afraid of bugs, and Clarisse didn't look like she was trying to make people start liking her. Maybe I just had to be okay with being afraid of swimming.

I heard the front door open and Momma call out, "I'm home."

Annette got up from the table, and I followed. Clarisse didn't move. Just as I reached the kitchen door, Clarisse grabbed my hand.

"Squirrels," she said.

"What?" I said, thinking I hadn't heard her right.

"I'm scared of squirrels too."

I opened my mouth and she said, "Remember when we stayed that summer with Uncle Kent?" I nodded yes. "And sometimes I would go in the house saying I was too hot to be outside?" I nodded yes again. "It wasn't because I was hot. It was because of those squirrels. Look like big ole rats with bushy tails. I thought I was gonna faint every time I saw one."

Clarisse smiled big. "But that's our little secret," she said to me.

I walked out to meet Momma laughing so hard, she must have thought I lost my mind.

FORTY

When Langston told me his daddy had him staying in all the next Saturday to make up for the chores he missed last week, I didn't tell him I wasn't going to the library either. I found out from Annette there was another swim meet, and I packed up my satchel like I always did when I was heading off to the library, but then I turned down Wabash and went straight to DuSable High.

I went early this time, and when I walked into the pool area, the first person I saw was Anthony.

"Annette's brother," he said, smiling that bright smile.

"Hey, Anthony." I smiled back. "Annette says to tell you good luck today," I told him, even though Annette didn't say nothing like that.

"She did?" he asked.

He walked over. Now that I knew all of the events, I asked him, "What are you swimming?"

"Just the freestyle and the relay," he said. "Both second heat." *Heat* wasn't something I knew. He could probably tell by my face.

"Fastest swimmers are in the first heats, slowest swimmers come in the heats after," he said. "I'm the slowest."

"You looked fast," I told him.

He hit my arm. "That's 'cause you don't swim." He laughed. "Oh... sorry 'bout that," he said.

"It's all right," I said. "Good luck."

"Look for the last person getting out the pool." Anthony laughed again. "That'll be me. Oh, and stick around after, I gotta talk to you about something."

Annette wasn't lying when she said the DuSable team was the best in the state. It looked like the DuSable swimmers beat the other swimmers by a mile in every heat. And Anthony might have been the slowest person on the DuSable team, but he wasn't the slowest in the pool. I stood up to watch when he swam his freestyle. He stretched his whole body out and just as soon as the tip of his finger touched the wall, he flipped over, pushed off, and did it again. He finished third in his free-style heat, behind two other DuSable swimmers but ahead of the other team, and second in the relay. By the time the meet ended, my throat was sore with all the screaming I was doing, and my back hurt from leaning forward in the hard seats. DuSable won again and just like the last time, everybody ran into the locker room and left the coach out at the pool cleaning up. Only this time, Anthony stayed behind too.

"Me and Mr. Thurber will take care of this, Coach," Anthony told him. The coach looked like he was happy to hear it.

"You boys sure?" he asked us.

I nodded yes, glad to be helping at the pool again.

Me and Anthony worked quick. I unhooked the lane lines and rolled them up. I picked up the towels and goggles. Anthony moved the benches near the wall and when everything was all straightened up, he came over and thanked me.

"Good job, Annette's brother." He gave me skin. "So, I got a little deal for you," he said, sitting down on the bench.

"I'm listening," I told him.

"Now, I ain't the best swimmer. But Coach says, I keep working, he could see me one day swimming in college. Maybe even get a scholarship by the time I'm a senior." Why someone would be swimming in college I didn't know, but I didn't want to stop him.

"So I was thinking…didn't you tell me you don't know how to swim?"

"Yup," I said.

"Well, I can teach you," he said.

I looked at him sideways.

"Nah," I told him. "I don't think anyone can teach me how to swim."

"I said the same thing," he said. "Until I didn't."

I stopped listening and kept shaking my head.

He reached out. "But you gotta do me a favor, though."

I stopped shaking my head.

"Annette," he said.

"Annette?"

"Yeah. You gotta put in a good word for me with your sister," Anthony said.

Now I laughed.

"You think Annette cares what good word her little brother is putting in?" I laughed again. "I may as well jump in the pool right now and drown."

"Wait a minute now," he said. "I can tell you're a smart dude. You just gotta be smooth. I have an older sister too. Trust me, this can work."

He looked so sure, I almost believed him.

"I can't do it," I told him.

"Not even for love?" he asked, putting his hand over his heart and blinking his long eyelashes fast.

"Oh, now it's love? Annette said you were only in her math class."

"Did she tell you I'm in French Club too?" he asked.

"So?"

"I will have you know I'm the only young man in the French Club," he said. "And it ain't because I love *le Français*."

"You really *are* in love," I said.

"I'll take that as a *oui*?" Anthony said, blinking his eyelashes again. Listening to him speak French like Annette made me think maybe they would make a nice boyfriend and girlfriend.

"And you really think you can teach me to swim?" I asked him.

"Absolutely," he said, looking serious. "First time I got in the pool"—he laughed, shaking his head—"I was splashing and kicking so bad, they had to pull me up out of there. Go on and get changed."

"Wait. Now?" I asked him.

"You don't ever want to wait till you have to. 'Cause then it may be too late," Anthony said, looking serious. "I just got hired as a lifeguard at the YMCA over on Wabash."

I never met anyone who was a lifeguard. "You ever have to save anyone?" I asked him.

"Not yet, and I don't want you to be the first one, Annette's brother," he said.

"How did you get a lifeguard job if you're not a good swimmer?" I asked, half believing him.

"Well, first off, I was being modest," he said, laughing. "I may not be the *fastest* swimmer, but that don't make me a *bad* swimmer. Huge difference. And second, I had to pass a lifeguard test. Which I did"—he flashed that big white smile—"with flying colors."

I'd bet Anthony could give Aunt Dorcas a run for her

money in the classroom. But he sounded like he was telling the truth.

"And I had to quit my other job to take the lifeguard job. Now you gonna ask me questions all day or do you want to learn to swim?"

"What was your other job?" I couldn't stop asking questions.

"So I guess you really don't want to learn to swim," Anthony said, still smiling. "I was a paper boy. Had my own route since I was younger than you."

"You make a lot of money as a paper boy?" I asked. I kept promising myself I was gonna stop asking Anthony questions, but something about him made me keep asking more. I wondered if I was trying to get as much information as I could so I could use it to torment Annette when I got home. But I remembered seeing those paper boys marching in the Bud Billiken Parade behind the big shot Abbott in his fancy white car.

"You ever march in the Bud Billiken Parade?"

"Course I did!" Anthony just about yelled. The sound in the room made echoes off the walls. "I was always right up front. Played trumpet in the newsboy band. You see me?"

How Anthony thought I would recognize him from the Bud Billiken Parade I don't know, but I nodded my head.

"Maybe," I said.

"All right, enough of this small talk," Anthony said. "Over there in my bag is an extra set of trunks." He pointed to the bench against the wall. "They may be a little big, but pull the string tight at the waist and they'll get the job done. Go get changed in the locker room. I'll be waiting."

"Coach ain't gonna mind you teaching me to swim?" I asked him.

He looked around the pool deck. "You see a coach in here?"

I walked to the bench and went to get the swim trunks.

FORTY-ONE

All the way home from my first swim lesson with Anthony I thought about my daddy. How I spent all these years looking at his pictures and hearing stories about how strong and brave he was and thinking that there was no one in the world less like my daddy than me. I thought if my daddy was alive to see the war end and come home to Chicago like all the other soldiers and daddies, he'd be ashamed to have a son so afraid to get into water he threw up on himself, wet the bed, and spent one whole week with his face in the water crying like a baby. But today, with Anthony holding on to my stomach underneath the water and my arms and legs stretched long like his and goggles on so the water didn't sting my eyes, and the water feeling good, I started thinking maybe my daddy could be proud of me after all.

Before we started our second lesson, Anthony told me we had to make sure it was okay with Coach Palmer for him to give me lessons, because he wasn't about to get kicked off the team for breaking rules. We both went into Coach's office, where he was sitting at a desk piled high with papers and schedules and equipment.

"How can I help you, boys?" he said, barely looking up.

I always thought of myself as a smooth talker, but by the time Anthony finished telling Coach Palmer how he wanted to help me to learn to swim, because I was afraid of water, though I wasn't sure he needed to tell him all that, about his time as a lifeguard and how surely Coach recognized how important it was for the Negro race to enter the sport of swimming, and how I would be a DuSable Sea Horse swimmer as soon as I started high school, I was thinking if Anthony didn't swim in college, he could definitely be a politician with a mouth like that. Coach must have thought so too because he could barely get a word in. Every time he said, "Well now…" Anthony added in something else. In ten minutes, Coach agreed to let Anthony teach me as long as my parents agreed and as long as Anthony abided by all the safety rules. When Anthony started in on how seriously he took his duty as a lifeguard, the coach just about shoved us out the door to get Anthony to stop talking.

"And that is how it's done, my man," Anthony said to me outside Coach's office, laughing as we walked back to the pool for our second lesson.

Once we started, Anthony taught me how to bend my arms like he did for my strokes and keep all my fingers together like I was making a cup. If he wasn't holding me up, for just a minute, I could pretend I was on the swim team too, imagining I looked like a real swimmer. Like my daddy.

And I thought that all the way home and up the stairs until I opened the door and saw my momma.

"Where have you been!" she shouted like I hadn't heard her shout before.

Only then did I notice how late it was. "I...was at the library," I said soft, hating the lie as soon as it left my mouth.

"Clemson Thurber Junior. God hates liars. I just sent your sisters out to look for you. Do you know what time it is?"

I shook my head no.

"Of course you don't. Because you don't care that I have been climbing the walls worried about where you were. That you are supposed to go the library and come straight back home. That I don't know how—"

"I was at the pool," I said, looking at Momma.

"I just told you, Clemson. God don't like liars. First Clarisse running her mouth at teachers and now you lying? Every day I've got to work for those trifling white folks, knowing that I'm trying on my own to make a better way. You think this is easy for me, Clem?" Momma sat down, holding her head.

I sat down next to her.

"I wish your daddy were here," she said. "I can't do it..."

"Momma," I told her. "I'm not lying. I was at the pool. Learning to swim."

She looked at me.

"I did lie about the library because I didn't think you'd let me go to the high school for the swim meet by myself. But Annette has a friend there named Anthony, who is sweet on Annette, but don't tell her I told you that part. Anyhow, he's on the swim team, but he's kind of the worst one on the swim team. But he likes Annette, but he also likes me too. He's a lifeguard at the YMCA, so he would never let me drown, and Coach says if you say—"

"Slow down, Clem," Momma said. "Take a breath."

Momma always tells me that when I'm trying to get too much of a story out at one time.

I went slower and told her everything about me seeing the swim team when she went to see the principal, and then me and Langston going to the swim meet, and then meeting Anthony. But I didn't tell her about what Anthony asked about putting in a good word with Annette in exchange for the lessons, and him being in love and all that, but I did tell her he said he'd help me.

Momma smiled just a little then. "And so?" she asked.

"So what?"

"Did you learn?"

"Not yet," I told her. "But I didn't feel scared like the other times."

Momma leaned in and hugged me. "Your daddy would be so proud of you, Clem," she said. "Knowing you were following in his footsteps. You are gonna make one heck of a navy man after all."

I held her arms and pulled back to look at her.

"Am I like my daddy?" I asked her.

Momma tilted her head to the side and looked at me, not answering.

I never asked my momma much about my daddy because I didn't want to see her sad. But one thing I knew was that I wasn't like Langston, feeling like I was just like my momma.

"Do I remind you of Daddy?" I asked. For the first time not caring if she got sad, but wanting, needing to know.

Finally, she said soft, "In some ways."

"What ways?" Looking at Momma, I could tell she'd rather be talking about anything but what we were talking about, but I was still holding on to her arms, not letting go.

I could see her eyes filling up. "You are funny like your daddy. He loved to laugh and joke. Too much sometimes." She smiled a little bit. "And you are both kindhearted. Not a mean bone in your body." I could feel something warm spreading over me, thinking that I shared a part of him my sisters didn't. Annette wasn't funny, and Clarisse sure wasn't kindhearted. That was all me.

I let go of Momma's arms and she stood up. I don't think she wanted to talk any more about Daddy, but I'd heard all I needed for now.

"Thank you, Momma," I said.

She wiped her eyes and nodded.

"He loved maps too," she said, and covered her mouth, turning fast to walk into the kitchen.

"Momma…" I didn't follow her.

I sat back on the couch thinking about what Momma told me about my daddy and how maybe the two of us needed time to be alone with our thoughts of him.

FORTY-TWO

I was sitting on the front steps of the school waiting for Langston when Errol came out. For years we spent just about every minute walking to and from school, eating lunch and out at recess, and now we acted like we barely knew each other. We always made sure to nod hello, but we were just as likely to pretend we didn't see each other. But today, sitting on the steps, when Errol came rushing out with Roland Carter and another boy I didn't know, I had to move out the way for them to get by. Errol and Roland nodded hello, and I nodded back. They started out across the school yard, but I saw Errol lean in and say something to Roland and then Errol doubled back. When he got to the steps, he stopped in front of me.

"You heard about Lymon?" he said.

"Lymon? No. What happened?" I was used to Lymon missing school for sometimes a week at a time. I noticed it more when we were the Three Musketeers. But now, spending most of my time with Langston, I barely noticed whether he was in school or not.

"He got sent to Arthur J. Audy Home," Errol said.

"The juvie home?" I asked him. "Where'd you hear that?" Lymon was bad, but not Arthur J. Audy Home bad.

"Roland's older brother told us," Errol said. I knew Roland's older brother was juvie bad.

I shook my head. "For what?" I asked him, feeling bad for not noticing he'd been missing.

Errol shrugged his shoulders. "All right, catch you later," he said.

I wondered how Lymon would make it in Arthur J. Audy. If he'd finally be scared in there with boys so much bigger and meaner than he could ever be. I knew it wasn't the fight with Langston that landed him in there, but I worried it was something worse. Every mad feeling I ever had about Lymon just disappeared then. I thought about him showing up to school beaten up and I wondered if Lymon would have to be fighting his whole life.

I watched Errol walking away with Roland and the new boy. The new Three Musketeers.

"Hey, you ready?" Langston asked, coming down the steps.

"Yup, let's go," I said, standing up.

We started off toward Michigan Avenue and the library.

That night at dinner, I helped Annette with the supper dishes.

"How are your swim lessons going?" she asked me.

"Well, Anthony's—"

"Clem, do *not* tell me a story about Anthony tonight. Please."

So instead of telling her all about how good of a teacher Anthony was, I told her how this week was the first time I swam without Anthony holding on to me.

"Congratulations. You signing up for the navy next week?" Annette laughed.

I was quiet then, with just the squeaky sound of the dish towel drying the plates.

"Suppose I don't want to join the navy?" I asked her. "You think Momma would be mad?"

"Mad? Why would Momma be mad?"

"Because she wants me to be a navy man like Daddy," I told her.

Annette turned off the water.

"Clem. Momma wants you to be happy. And if that means not being a navy man, then don't join the navy. But how do you know you don't want to join?" she asked me.

"Well, I know I love swimming. And I want to travel and visit all the places I see on maps. But I don't want to fight, Annette. I don't have it in me."

"Then why even bother learning to swim?"

"I don't know, so I'm not afraid anymore, I guess," I said. "So I can feel brave."

Annette tilted her head to the side, looking at me. "You don't have to swim to feel brave."

"Maybe *you* don't have to swim to feel brave," I told her. "I do."

Annette handed me a plate to dry. "Is this because of Daddy?" she asked.

"I think it was at first," I said. "Now I think…"

Annette waited.

"I think I'm just tired of being scared."

Annette nodded.

"I know you don't remember much about Daddy," she said. "But as brave as he was, I'd bet you a lot of times, he was still scared."

"So you're saying even if I learn to swim and join the swim team and become the top swimmer on the DuSable swim team, I could still be scared sometimes?" I asked her.

"I guess we'll have to wait and see," she said, smiling.

FORTY-THREE

It was the first time in weeks Momma got home so early me and Clarisse were still in the kitchen doing our schoolwork.

"Well, isn't this a sight for sore eyes?" Momma said, putting the grocery sack on the table.

I got up to help but Clarisse didn't move, her face in her history book.

"Hi, Momma," she said, not looking up. "I have a history exam tomorrow."

"Well, study away," Momma said, taking off her coat and heading back out front to hang it up.

When she came back in she asked, "Annette's at her club?"

"Yup," I answered, since I knew Clarisse wouldn't.

And that reminded me. "Momma, did I tell you that Anthony says he wants to swim in college?"

"Oh?" Momma said. "You hear that, Clarisse? Anthony's going to be a college boy. You are going to meet some fine young men when you head off to Howard University after you graduate next year."

"Mmmhmmm," Clarisse said, her head still in her history book.

"Clarisse, why do you do that every time I mention

Howard?" Momma said. "I know your aunts Dorcas and Bethel talked to you about the opportunities there. With your grades, I don't think you'd have any problem getting in."

"Mmmhmmm," Clarisse said, still not looking up.

I could see a frown starting on Momma's face, and I knew I wasn't going to get my schoolwork finished tonight if Clarisse got Momma all worked up.

"Clarisse," Momma said, trying not to sound mad, "please look at me when I'm speaking to you."

Clarisse looked up at Momma.

"Is there another college you were thinking of attending?" Momma asked.

"You mean one that doesn't cost any money?" Clarisse said, looking Momma dead in her face.

"What exactly does that mean, Clarisse?"

"Last time I checked, colleges weren't free. We can barely keep the lights on with what the Franklins pay you, how am I supposed to go to college?" Clarisse's mouth turned up at the corners in a little smile when she finished.

Momma breathed in deep. "Well, I never knew you were so worried about how much the Franklins were paying me, Clarisse. But if it's money you're concerned about, I planned to put aside the money from your father's settlement when it comes in and use it toward college for the three of you. I think we'll be okay if—"

"You mean *if* it comes in. It's been years, Momma. How long are you going to keep waiting?" Clarisse put her head back down and kept right on flipping through the pages of her history book. "Besides, it's not just the money. I don't need to go to some school all the way in Washington, D.C., just because you and your uppity sisters think I'm too good for schools in Chicago."

It felt like my heart stopped beating. Now things were getting too good for me to go anywhere. I put down my pencil and looked up at Momma and then at Clarisse, making sure to remember every word to tell Annette later.

"What did you just say to me, Clarisse?" Momma asked her, soft as a whisper, which was almost worse than shouting. Then Momma did something she never does. She just about yelled, "I'm talking to you!"

Clarisse looked up quick. "I don't want to go to Howard or any of those fancy schools you and your sisters want me to go to. I'm going to stay right here in Chicago. Besides, I'm not leaving Ralph."

Momma took a deep breath and shook her head. Her voice was soft again. "Well, I don't know who this Ralph is, but he is certainly not someone who is going to decide your future. And Howard is not just one of 'those fancy schools,' Clarisse. It is one of the most—"

"Ralph is my boyfriend."

Momma leaned forward. I could see she was trying to keep her temper, but the way Clarisse was going tonight, I wasn't sure how long that would last. "You are not allowed to have a boyfriend, Clarisse. Especially one who doesn't value education."

"Ralph values education. He's going to play basketball for Crane Junior College, and I promised him I'd wait for him. Right here. In Chicago." Clarisse looked up in Momma's eyes and smiled her Pontiac smile right in her face.

Momma waited. I think she was praying to God she didn't kill Clarisse with her bare hands, and I was praying right along with her. God must have answered her prayers because she kept on talking soft.

"I was scared too when I went off to school and I only went down the street from my momma and daddy." Momma stepped closer to Clarisse. "Going to college is the only chance you're going to have in this world to get ahead, Clarisse, you've got to trust me—"

Clarisse stood up, staring into Momma's eyes. "How did college ever help you get ahead?" Clarisse was shouting now. "Get ahead? You mean like you? *A maid?*" The way Clarisse said *maid* sounded like she spit the word in Momma's face.

Momma slapped Clarisse so fast and hard I thought I was seeing things. Seeing that made me feel like I was in the school yard with Lymon and Errol and Langston and even Curtis all over again and me just sitting there watching, doing nothing. But the Clem who stood there watching in the school yard wasn't the same Clem who got in the pool with Anthony, splashing like a fool but remembering to move my arms and kick my legs to keep me moving just a little bit more every week. It was the Clem who wasn't brave yet but was maybe just a little bit less afraid.

The only time I'd ever seen Momma look this mad was when Errol's momma was in our apartment crying over what Errol's daddy did to her. When Momma raised her hand to slap Clarisse again, I shouted, "Momma, no!" I jumped up from the table and reached out, grabbing Momma's arm. Both Momma and Clarisse looked at me.

"Stop," I said. Softer this time, not letting go of Momma's arm.

Momma dropped her arm and tears ran down her cheeks. Clarisse's too. Clarisse's face had a red mark from where Momma had slapped her, and she reached up to touch it. I could see black makeup running down Clarisse's cheeks all mixed in with her tears, and all I could think was that if I let go of Momma's hand she was going to hit Clarisse extra for wearing makeup when she wasn't supposed to.

"If your daddy were here…," Momma said soft through her teeth. She still sounded mad, so I held her hand some more.

"Well, he ain't here, Momma! He ain't here. He ain't never gonna be here again." I never knew Clarisse could cry so hard. Like the tears wouldn't stop.

Momma pulled her hand away from mine and went to hold Clarisse, but Clarisse pushed her away.

"He's gone," Clarisse said. "He's gone, Momma. Daddy's gone."

Momma tried again to hold her, and this time Clarisse just stood still, letting Momma's arm wrap around her. Clarisse laid her head on the front of Momma's uniform so her cries sounded like her head was buried in a pillow. I stood and watched, wondering if there was anything I should say. But I made myself be quiet. Momma laid her head on top of Clarisse's and they rocked back and forth, Momma rubbing Clarisse's back and shushing her.

We looked a mess, the three of us standing there in the middle of our kitchen. No one knowing what to say. So when Annette walked in the kitchen, we couldn't have been happier to see her.

FORTY-FOUR

"Clarisse said what?" Me and Annette were in the kitchen late after Momma and Clarisse had gone to bed. I needed to tell Annette everything that happened, step by step, like we were at the motion pictures.

"And then she said, 'Ralph is my boyfriend.'"

"Clemson Thurber, you are lying!" Annette said, whispering and laughing at the same time.

When I told her about the part where Clarisse called Momma a maid, Annette said, "Well, I would have slapped her too," looking almost as mad as Momma.

"I don't think Clarisse is gonna mess with Momma again," I told Annette, and she laughed again, but then we remembered we were supposed to be whispering.

"I'm not even sure Clarisse meant any of what she was saying. It sounded like she was just sad about Daddy," I said.

"Mmmmhmmm," Annette said, nodding her head.

"You knew Clarisse was upset about Daddy?" I asked her.

"Clem, sometimes I wonder how you were skipped a grade if you are so dumb."

"How was I supposed to know? She never even talks about Daddy," I said, my voice getting loud.

"Did you know I miss Daddy too?" Annette said.

And then I did feel dumb. Momma hardly ever talked about Daddy, but I could see the way she got sad sometimes thinking about him. I guess Annette was right that you don't always have to say how you're feeling just to be feeling it. I shrugged. "You do?"

Annette leaned toward me. "I know you don't remember much about him, but me and Clarisse do. He used to take us everywhere with him, like we were his pride and joy. He'd say 'You see my angels' to just about everyone we passed on the street. And it was like Christmas every time he got home from one of his train runs. He had gifts for us in every pocket. Momma said he was spoiling us, but he didn't care. I can still smell his aftershave." Annette stopped. The only person who cries less than Clarisse is Annette, so after seeing Clarisse cry today, I didn't know what to expect, but Annette's eyes stayed dry. "He would always mash his face up against ours after he came from the barbershop. 'Is Daddy smooth or what?' he'd ask us, and we would rub his face…" Annette looked up at the ceiling. "He always smelled so good. Seemed like when he was here, Momma was always happy. They used to dance, right in there." She pointed to the front room. "And then Daddy would take turns dancing with us too. When we lost Daddy, we lost part of Momma too. The best part. But when Momma looks at you, she sees Daddy and that keeps her going. Maybe we all do."

If I had something to ask when Annette started talking, I didn't now. This picture of my daddy, I'd never see in a picture frame or by watching my momma look out a window. My daddy dancing and laughing was the Daddy I wished I knew. But I could never miss him like they did because it was hard to miss something I never had.

I could see Clarisse's face after Momma slapped her. And hear her crying how Daddy was gone. Now I knew the hurt we all were feeling. Each in our own way.

"I'm sorry, Annette," I said.

"Sorry for what?"

"Sorry for not noticing."

In the dim light of the kitchen, Annette looked so tired. She rubbed my hand like Momma sometimes did. "Thank you, Clem. Maybe you're not so dumb after all."

FORTY-FIVE

Anthony told me we only had one more lesson before the season ended, and I tried to act like it didn't make any difference to me, but swimming with Anthony was almost as good as going to the library every Saturday. Maybe better.

At home I talked about Anthony so much, Annette asked me if I was in love with him.

"He's just a good teacher. You'd probably like him," I said, and remembering my promise to Anthony, I added in, "as a boyfriend."

"When I need dating advice from you, I'll let you know," Annette told me, but she usually didn't mind listening to my stories about how Anthony was helping me to swim.

"I tried," I told Anthony during our last lesson. "I told you, she's not going to listen to me."

"Don't worry, I got another plan," Anthony said.

We started warming up with stretches and the kickboard. And then Anthony watched as I practiced my freestyle.

"You are so good now, you might just beat me," he said, smiling.

I smiled, wishing that was true.

"I was thinking, because it's our last day, we should have a kind of a celebration," Anthony said.

"Like cake and ice cream?" I asked, laughing.

"Nah, like our own swim meet."

"Just me and you?" I asked, thinking Anthony must be out of his mind.

I heard a door open, and I looked up scared, thinking it was Coach, coming to watch. I swam over to the edge of the pool, thinking if Coach saw me swimming now, he'd never let me on the swim team in high school. But it wasn't Coach. It was Annette. And Clarisse and Momma. And that made me more scared than seeing the coach.

"What—"

"What do you think, Annette's brother? Wanna race?" Anthony asked.

I couldn't make my mouth close.

"Your sister wanted to see your first swim meet," Anthony said.

"You invited Annette here?" I said, grabbing the ladder to get out of the pool.

"Nah, nah," he said, grabbing my arm. "I promised to teach you to swim, and I did. You promised to make me look good in front of your sister. This is your chance. She sees you can swim, she's gonna fall in love with me for sure." Anthony laughed. "I guess she brought company."

Momma waved from the end of the pool.

"Come on, just don't beat me too bad," Anthony said. From where I stood, it looked like Clarisse was already rolling her eyes, expecting me to drown and waste everyone's time.

I climbed down the ladder and stood in the pool again.

I stared at the water in front of me. With Anthony I only swam from side to side, never the whole length of the pool and into the deep part.

"It's only twenty-five yards," Anthony said. "You could doggy-paddle twenty-five yards."

It looked like a lot more than twenty-five yards to me. It looked like an ocean.

I touched my stomach. But before I started wondering if it was going to start up again, Anthony yelled out, "Annette!"

She looked over at us and waved.

"Start us off," Anthony said. He looked over at me and winked. "I'll be right here next to you, Annette's brother."

I dropped my hands to my sides and looked straight ahead.

"Ready. Set. Go!" Annette yelled from the end of the pool.

We both pushed off from the wall.

I started slow, thinking about all Anthony had taught

me, about my arms, legs, breathing, and head turning, and once I got all those things going together and realized I was moving, only then did I think about racing Anthony. He was going slow, I could tell, staying with me until I got myself together, and when I turned my head, there he was right at my side, smiling his big smile.

"C'mon, Clem," I could hear, fuzzy-sounding through the water. I didn't know if it was my momma, Clarisse, Annette, or all three of them, and I didn't care, I just knew I was swimming side by side with Anthony. My arms turned in time with his and my head turned to the side just as his was turning away, and for just one second, I saw my daddy, swimming right alongside me. I moved my arms faster and then as fast as I could make them, but Anthony started pulling away. I knew I was in the deep part, right in the middle of the pool. I didn't look down. My head moved from side to side, and I was breathing in and out, in rhythm. Pretty soon I wasn't looking at Anthony's head, but at the bottoms of his feet through the splashing water, but I didn't care. I wasn't thinking anymore about making my arms and legs move, it was like they knew just what to do, so I kept on swimming, not stopping until my hand hit the wall of the pool.

I grabbed the ledge and lifted my head, breathing hard and spitting out water. My chest felt like it was on fire. Everybody, even Anthony, was clapping. He was looking at

Annette, but Annette and Momma and Clarisse were looking at me. I turned back and looked all the way down to the end of the pool where the starting blocks were. Twenty-five yards. *An ocean.* That may not seem like a long way for most folks, but for me, my momma, and my sisters, it felt like I just swam from here to the San Francisco Bay.

FORTY-SIX

Momma, Annette, and Clarisse talked with Anthony while I changed out of my swim trunks and back into my clothes. I could tell right away that Momma was impressed with how polite and smart Anthony was. It helped that Anthony was doing a lot of "Well, the pleasure was all mine, Mrs. Thurber" and "What a lovely family you have, Mrs. Thurber." That last one he said looking at Annette. By the time I made my way back to them Anthony was saying, "Just give me a minute to change," and running to the locker room.

"Anthony is going to join us for supper," Momma said to me, smiling. I looked over at Annette, but she was quiet. Clarisse hid her laugh behind her hand.

On the walk home, Momma walked close to me. "Clem, for a minute, I thought you were going to beat Anthony, you were swimming so fast," she said, laughing.

"He slowed down for me, Momma," I told her.

"I am just...just so proud of you," Momma said. I was expecting her to start wiping at her eyes, but when I looked up at her, she was smiling and happy. Like for the first time, she saw just me and not the part that reminds her of my daddy.

While Momma was cooking dinner, Me and Anthony, Annette, and Clarisse sat in the front room. Annette was quiet but that didn't slow down Anthony's talking. He had all kinds of stories about his family, swim team, his plans to work at a camp for the summer. He and Clarisse even talked about college, and me and Annette almost fell over when Clarisse told Anthony she would most likely be attending Howard University.

"They have a good swim team," she told him. "You should apply."

By the time Momma called us in for dinner, he was telling us a story about a close call with a dog chasing him on his paper route.

"So you also have a paper route?" Momma asked him.

"Not anymore, ma'am. I had to give it up when I got my lifeguard job down at the YMCA," he said.

We bowed our heads in prayer and Anthony reached out to hold Annette's hand. Before we closed our eyes, he winked at me.

"Well, you are certainly very enterprising," Momma said to Anthony. "A paper route and now a lifeguard."

"Yes ma'am," Anthony said, helping himself to mashed potatoes. "I'm saving for college."

Momma looked over at Clarisse. One thing I know is that Clarisse didn't care if we had company or not, she would say whatever she felt like saying back to Momma, so I jumped in. "How do you get a paper route?" I asked Anthony.

"Well, you have to head down to the *Chicago Defender* office and talk to…" Anthony stopped. "Unless"—his mouth was full of food—"you want to take over my old route?" he asked.

"Your old route?" All this time I'd been feeling like no one ever felt that I had something to contribute. Maybe now with a paper route, I could.

"Sure. The route's not far from here. You got to be an early riser, though, and—"

"I'm an early riser, right, Momma?" I said, looking at Momma.

"Well, yes, but—"

"That's half the battle right there. Getting up early, getting all your papers folded and ready to go. You'll be finished with delivery by the time everybody else is just getting up. And then you head off to school. And the money's not bad," Anthony said, reaching for another piece of chicken.

Finally, Annette spoke. "Thanks, Anthony, but I don't know if that's for Clem," she said. "Not just yet."

"Why isn't it?" I asked her.

Everyone was quiet, and all we could hear was the sound of Anthony chewing.

Anthony helped himself to thirds and kept talking like he didn't notice everyone else was quiet. After he thanked Momma about a thousand times for dinner and her "gracious hospitality," Annette finally saw him out.

I had plenty of time to think while Clarisse and Momma started clearing the table. And even more while I waited until the last plate was cleared and the pots were in the sink soaking. And when Annette came back into the kitchen and Momma said to her, "That Anthony sure is sweet on you," I stood up.

"I'm doing it," I told them.

"Doing what exactly?" Clarisse said, looking bored.

"The paper route."

"Now, Clem. I know how much you admire Anthony," Momma said. "We all do—"

"Especially Annette," Clarisse said, smiling over at her.

"Not now, Clarisse," Momma told her. "Clem, I appreciate your wanting to take on more responsibility, but I don't think—"

"Momma, I'm taking over Anthony's paper route. Anthony told me he started his when he was younger than me. I'm up early anyhow. I'll deliver the papers and be back in time for school."

"Clem, I think what Momma is trying to say is that you are still—"

"A baby? A little boy? Someone who can't be trusted with anything? Someone who will get hurt if I'm not with my momma?"

"Yes," Clarisse said.

"Clarisse!" Momma and Annette yelled at the same time.

"But Clarisse is right, isn't she? That's exactly what you all think," I said. I thought I'd feel like crying. But just like Kendrick said, I was too mad to let one tear go. I stood up straight.

"If I'm a baby, it's because you all won't let me be nothing else," I said, leaving out to go to my room.

The next morning, we were quiet all through breakfast. Momma kissed me goodbye as she grabbed her purse.

"Clem," she said soft, looking into my eyes. "I'm not trying to treat you like a baby." I waited. "I'm just trying to make sure you're safe is all. You understand that, right?" I nodded. "Let's talk when I get home," Momma said, kissing me once more on top of my head before she left.

I walked downstairs, past Errol's apartment. It seemed like a million years ago that we walked to school together every day. Up ahead, I could see Langston waiting for me at the corner and I hurried to catch up.

"That math homework was so hard last night, I thought my brain was going to catch fire," Langston said, laughing, when I started walking beside him.

Langston could tell something was wrong the way I didn't have a whole lot to add.

We walked a little further and then he asked, "What's wrong?"

And everything came out at once. "Whoa, slow down. Alabama style," Langston said, smiling. He reminded me of Momma telling me to take my time telling a story. So I told it as slow as I could. So slow, we had to wait outside the school until the bell rang so I could finish.

"And I am sick and tired of being treated like a baby when I'm not."

"So that's what's wrong," Langston said to me.

"That's all you got?" I just about yelled.

"Well, if you're looking for me to give you an answer, wouldn't I be treating you like a baby too?"

Standing right here in front of me was my answer from the mouth of a country boy from Alabama, who happened to be one of the smartest people I knew.

FORTY-SEVEN

I thought I knew early morning in Chicago when I got up early with Momma and the light was just starting to come in through the windows. The city was so quiet then, like it was stuck in a game of freeze tag. But that early morning is nothing like the early morning of my paper route. It was the first time I woke up before Momma, walking quiet past her sleeping on the couch on my way to the bathroom to wash up. I got dressed every day in the clothes I laid out on my bed the night before, so I didn't have to open and close any drawers or turn on the lights. The last thing I did before I left out every morning was take out the knife Kendrick gave me from under my mattress where I hid it since I got back from Milwaukee. I slipped that into my back pocket and headed out the front door.

Cutting the twine wrapped around the papers I folded for my route was all I needed my knife for, but feeling it my pocket reminded me of Kendrick and how there wasn't much that scared him. I wished he could see me now, going door-to-door in the dark in Chicago, by myself delivering papers. I know I'll probably never be like Kendrick, but I know too that just because I'm scared doesn't mean I can't feel brave too.

After Anthony spoke to his boss at the *Defender* about me taking over his route, all I had to do was to go on downtown and shake hands with the newspaperman who was the boss over all the paper boys, get my addresses and my list of customers. It was like learning to swim all over again with Anthony going over each step until I was sure I had it and could do it on my own. He even wrote down his address on a piece of paper and told me he lived near my route. "If anything happens, knock on the door, and I'll be there," he told me. I'm not sure if Anthony will ever get Annette to fall in love with him, but I'm always gonna be rooting for him. Anthony didn't know I made my own map, with every street on my route and an X marking off each house. I used it every day up until I could just about do my route with my eyes closed.

When Momma saw how nothing she said was going to make me change my mind about the paper route, and Annette told her Anthony was going to help me by going over everything, she agreed to "see how it works out." That was weeks ago and now it seemed no one barely noticed I was gone each morning and back in time for breakfast. My first pay wasn't much and as bad as I wanted to buy a stack of new Batman comics and a new map, I gave every penny to Momma.

"Clem, you earned this on your own, I can't take it,"

she said. But I put it in an envelope and left it on the table with her name on the front. When she opened it the next morning, she looked at me and smiled. "Are you my secret admirer?" she said, laughing, and then put it in her purse.

When I talked to Langston about my paper route and my map and all the stories I read in the paper each morning, he said, "You thinking about taking over Abbott's job one day? You could run the whole paper."

I had never in my life thought about running a newspaper until I started delivering them. Every morning, when I sat folding them, it took me twice as long as some of the other boys, at first because I needed to get the hang of the fold, but then, even after I figured how to fold them just right, I couldn't stop reading the stories. *Articles* they called them, from all around the world. It felt like traveling without ever leaving Chicago and made me wonder if I could be one of those *Defender* reporters traveling to all the places I've seen on my maps and writing stories from Japan and Europe. Having the time all to myself in early-morning Chicago was the part I wasn't looking forward to because it was the only time of the day when I had to be quiet. But with the quiet came time for me to think about things that my talking didn't let me think about. Things about Lymon, Errol, Langston, Kendrick, K.J., Clarisse, Annette, and Momma. But mostly things about me and Daddy.

Instead of thinking if my daddy would be proud of me doing this on my own and helping my family, I realized for once I wasn't thinking about my daddy, my momma, or my sisters. I was thinking how for the first time, I was proud of me. I wasn't sure if this was what bravery felt like or what responsibility felt like. But it sure felt good.

I was Clemson Thurber Junior. Clemson. Clem. I was all of those. Not half my daddy, but part him and part Momma too, but mostly me. I couldn't spend my time worrying about who I was supposed to be. I was finally happy with just being Clem.

Author's Note

Writing historical fiction allows me to research and explore periods from America's past that were never discussed in the classrooms of my youth. In *Finding Langston*, I boarded a train during the Great Migration, wandered alongside young Langston in the stacks of Chicago's Cleveland Hall Branch library and read the poetry of Langston Hughes. In *Leaving Lymon*, I traveled to Mississippi, heard the stories of prisoners in Parchman State Penitentiary, and sang along to the music of traveling blues musicians. And now, in *Being Clem*, the final book in the Finding Langston trilogy, I journeyed to San Francisco and the site of the Port Chicago Disaster and cheered as the Bud Billiken Parade marched by. In each of these journeys into the past, I am faced time and again, with the stories of people who in their quest for fairness, respect, and equality, were instead faced with injustice and discrimination. Yet the obstacles they encountered at every turn produced not just anger and frustration, rebellion and hurt, but more often determination, resilience, perseverance, creativity, joy, and love. Each of these books represents pieces of an often-overlooked history of Blacks in this country, and reminds me that through every hurt and pain Blacks have experienced, the strength of family and community remained intact.

On July 17, 1944, the fictional Clem Thurber's life was forever altered by the real-life events of the Port Chicago Disaster. Located in the San Francisco Bay, the Port Chicago naval base was home to hundreds of servicemen who had enlisted to serve their country during World War Two. Black men who joined the armed forces prepared to fight in service of their country were instead shipped to parts of the country to perform the most menial and dangerous tasks that white soldiers did not want to perform. At the Port Chicago base, Black soldiers loaded explosives, bombs, and ammunition from train cars onto ships that were then transported to the white forces fighting the Japanese in the Pacific.

Previously, white stevedores, or dock workers, who held this dangerous job, were provided with safety instruction and manuals. Yet white officers, believing Black sailors were unable to comprehend written manuals, offered none. The soldiers worked in shifts and devised their own methods to safely load the explosives. They rightly feared that one wrong move could result in their deaths.

On the evening of July 17, 1944, shortly after lights out in the barracks, a loud explosion reverberated through the base. Men scrambled, thinking they were being bombed by the enemy. The explosion was so strong, that some were lifted off of their mattresses as they slept, and the barracks collapsed around them.

In the early morning light, the devastation of the bomb blast became clear. The entire pier, along with the remains of the two ships, were blown to shreds. One of the ships had been carrying nearly ten million pounds of explosives. Black sailors were assigned the task of retrieving the body parts of the sailors who were aboard the ship from the Pacific Ocean, none of whom remained intact after the explosion. Of the three hundred people presumed to be at the waterfront when the explosion happened, only fifty-one bodies were able to be identified. And, of the 320 men killed, 202 of them were Black sailors who were on the evening shift, loading ammunition. Clem's father Clemson would have been one of the men who did not survive the blast.

Just months after the tragedy, surviving sailors were ordered to return to work. Some of the men, fearing retribution, did return. But fifty others, named the Port Chicago 50, refused to do so, and were court martialed and charged with mutiny for defying their commanding officer's orders. The penalty if found guilty: death by firing squad.

A young Black civil rights attorney for the NAACP named Thurgood Marshall, who had been traveling throughout the country representing discrimination cases of Black enlisted men, was called in to represent the men. Marshall had witnessed many cases of racism throughout the military. On some bases, Black soldiers had to wait to eat until white soldiers were served first. On others they had to clean the toilets in white barracks. Most often when the soldiers left the base for a day of liberty, they faced other threats from white residents in nearby cities who refused them service in restaurants and bars. The NAACP and Black newspapers throughout the country helped to publicize the stories of the Port Chicago 50 and thousands signed petitions to demand their release. Despite all of those efforts and the tireless work of Marshall, the men were found guilty. As they awaited their sentence, the war ended. On January 7, 1946, after sixteen months in prison, the U. S. Navy quietly released the men from prison and returned them to active duty. The U.S. Navy never admitted to wrongfully convicting the men. On July 26, 1948, President Truman signed an Executive Order desegregating the U.S. military. Thurgood Marshall went on to become the first African American Justice to serve on the United States Supreme Court.

The United States Congress wrote up legislation to compensate the families of the Black sailors with grants in the amount of $5,000, which in today's dollars would amount to approximately $72,000. However, one lone senator from Mississippi argued to have that amount reduced to $3,000 when he discovered that the victim's families were Black. The $3,000 amount was unanimously approved by Congress.

Clem's life in 1940's Chicago is enriched by a vibrant African American community. In 1905 Robert Sengstacke Abbott founded the *Chicago Defender* newspaper, which is still in print today. The *Defender* has been credited with increasing Chicago's Black population by promoting the advantages of life in the north to Blacks in the south. Often distributed by Black Pullman porters on their train routes, the *Defender* hired notable writers such as Gwendolyn Brooks, journalists Ethel Payne and Ida B. Wells, and poet Langston Hughes, who wrote a weekly column.

The Billiken was considered the guardian angel of children and a prominent feature of both the newspaper's children's column and the parade. Celebrated on the first Saturday of each August since 1929, the Bud Billiken Parade remains one of the longest running and largest African American parades in the country. Grand marshalls have included Cab Calloway, Muhammad Ali, Lena Horne, Oprah Winfrey, Barack Obama, and heavyweight champion Joe Louis.

It was at DuSable High school where Clem first learned to swim. In 1934, DuSable High School opened its doors at 4934 S. Wabash Avenue. It was one of the only high schools in the area built with a swimming pool and some white high school teams refused to compete against the all-Black team. Coach William T. Mackie, who once swam competitively was hired to run the DuSable swim program. Under Coach Mackie, the DuSable High Sea Horses became one the best teams in the state of Illinois through 1943 where they won fifty-three consecutive dual meets.

Lesa Cline-Ransome

Acknowledgments

Being Clem is the final chapter in a journey that began years ago with a manuscript I wasn't quite sure what to do with, but which fortunately found its way into the hands of my editor, Mary Cash, who thankfully knew exactly what it was meant to be. Thank you, Mary, for your vision. Not just for the first book, *Finding Langston*, but for knowing that Langston's story should continue into *Leaving Lymon* and now *Being Clem*, this final book in the trilogy. Thank you for bringing these characters' voices to life with your patience and gentle guidance. Thanks to everyone at Holiday House for making me feel like part of a family. Thank you to my agent, Rosemary Stimola, of Stimola Literary Studio, sage, twin, and fearless advocate.

Thank you to my dear friend Lisa Reticker, who after reading *Finding Langston* insisted it should be a trilogy and pushed me forward every step of the way. And to her husband, Mark Fuerst, who coached me in the reading of my Author's Note for the audiobook version. And speaking of audiobooks, thank you Dreamscape Media, and Dion Graham, narrator of all three titles, whose gifted voice found the heart and soul of Langston, Lymon, and Clem and the cast of characters that surrounded them. You are truly a genius.

I so appreciate the help of those along the way who helped me to find the answers to my obscure questions—Jay Dorin, Cathy and Rebecca Shaw, J.E. Williams, Linda Cline, Eduardo Vann, and Elizabeth Ascoli. Thanks to my wonderful writer's group, who offered invaluable critique along the way: Christine Heppermann, Virginia Euwer Wolff, Ann Burg, Julie Chibarro, Alyssa Wishingrad, Jocelyn Johnson-Kearney, Phoebe North, Gayle Upchurch-Mills, and Stephanie Tolan, who read and reread entire drafts and offered their invaluable insight when it was most needed.

And thank you to my wonderful family, who are so patient when I spend long hours in my office, order too much takeout, complain nonstop, and read aloud too many versions of the same chapter. You are all what keeps me going. Malcolm, thank you for your honesty and vulnerability in helping me to understand the challenges facing young black men (and for teaching me how to throw a rock); Leila, thank you for being a patient reader and fierce critic. Much gratitude to my hubby and jacket cover artist extraordinaire, James Ransome, for answering all of my questions about manhood and your childhood. Thanks to Maya and Jaime for your unwavering support. And to my mother Ernestine and my siblings, Linda and Bill Cline. The memories of our childhood are what helped to form the foundation for this story. You taught me to love life and follow my dreams and cheered me every step of the way when I did.

Lesa Cline-Ransome